MAKING BOMBS FOR HITLER

Marsha Forchuk Skrypuch

Scholastic Canada Ltd.
Toronto New York London Auckland Sydney
Mexico City New Delhi Hong Kong Buenos Aires

Scholastic Canada Ltd.
604 King Street West, Toronto, Ontario M5V 1E1, Canada

Scholastic Inc.
557 Broadway, New York, NY 10012, USA

Scholastic Australia Pty Limited
PO Box 579, Gosford, NSW 2250, Australia

Scholastic New Zealand Limited
Private Bag 94407, Botany, Manukau 2163, New Zealand

Scholastic Children's Books
Euston House, 24 Eversholt Street, London NW1 1DB, UK

www.scholastic.ca

Library and Archives Canada Cataloguing in Publication

Skrypuch, Marsha Forchuk, 1954-
Making bombs for Hitler / Marsha Forchuk Skrypuch.
ISBN 978-1-4431-0730-3

1. World War, 1939-1945–Children–Juvenile fiction.
2. World War, 1939-1945–Prisoners and prisons, German– Juvenile
fiction. 3. Sisters–Juvenile fiction. I. Title.

PS8587.K79M34 2012   jC813'.54   C2011-905482-5

Cover cameo: Eric Vega/istockphoto.
Cover cameo: Najim/Shutterstock.

6 5 4 3   Printed in Canada   139   13 14 15 16

For Anelia V.

Contents

Chapter One

Losing Larissa — 1943

The room smelled of soap and the light was so white that it made my eyes ache. I held Larissa's hand in a tight grip. I was her older sister after all, and she was my responsibility. It would be easy to lose her in this sea of children, and we had both lost far too much already. Larissa looked up at me and I saw her lips move but I couldn't hear her words above the wails and screams. I bent down so that my ear was level with her lips.

"Don't leave me," she said.

I wrapped my arms around her and gently rocked her back and forth. I whispered our favourite lullaby into her ear.

A loud crack startled us both. The room was suddenly silent. A woman in white stepped in among us. She clapped her hands sharply once more.

"Children," she said in brisk German. "You will each have a medical examination."

Weeping children were shoved into a long snaking line

that took up most of the room. I watched as one by one other children were taken behind a broad white curtain.

When it was Larissa's turn, her eyes went round with fright. I did not want to let go of her, but the nurse pulled our hands apart.

"Lida, stay with me."

I stood at the edge of the curtain and watched as the woman made Larissa take off her nightgown. My sister's face was red with shame. When the woman held a metal instrument to her face, Larissa screamed. I rushed up and tried to knock that thing out of the nurse's hand, but she called for help and someone held me back. When they finished with Larissa, they told her to stand at the other end of the room.

When it was my turn, I barely noticed what they were doing. I kept my eyes fixed on Larissa. She was standing with three other children. Dozens more had been ordered to stand in a different spot.

When the nurse was finished with me, I slipped my nightgown back on. I was ordered to stand with the larger group — not with Larissa's.

"I need to be in that group," I told the nurse, pointing to where Larissa stood, her arms outstretched, a look of panic on her face.

The nurse's lips formed a thin flat line. "No talking."

She put one hand on each of my shoulders and shoved me towards the larger group. A door opened wide. We were herded out into the blackness of night.

Larissa screamed, "Lida! Don't leave me!"

I looked back into the room, but could not see her. "I will find you, Larissa!" I shouted. "I promise. Stay strong."

A sharp slap across my face sent me sprawling onto the

cold wet grass. I scrambled up and tried to break through the sea of children. I had to get back to Larissa.

Strong arms wrapped around my torso and lifted me up. I was thrown into blackness. With a screech of metal the door slammed shut.

❖ ❖ ❖

Blackness.

I dreamed that I was lying in a sea of humming bees. We were swaying back and forth and I sang the lullaby under my breath, imagining that I was being rocked in Mama's arms. I opened my eyes. It was so dark they took a few minutes to adjust.

I was crammed inside a hot metal room that smelled like a dirty barn. It was so stuffy and stinky and crowded that I could barely breathe. I realized with a shock that we were moving. This was not a room after all, but a train car — the kind for cattle. It swayed back and forth. The sound was not the humming of bees, but the whispers of frightened children and the thrumming of the train on its tracks. At least the sound of war was muffled out.

"Does anyone know where we're going?"

The whispers stopped. A lone thin voice answered. "To Germany, I think."

My heart sank. If they took me to Germany, how would I ever find Larissa? Wherever she was, she must be feeling so frightened, so alone.

I tried to stand, but with the movement of the car and the hazy light, I fell backwards, one of my bare feet landing on another child's chest.

"Ow!" she cried.

"I am sorry."

It was pointless to try standing, so I sat up and tried to

get my bearings. In the dim light I could see a tangle of limbs and tufts of hair. Children were packed in so tightly that each overlapped the other. Something smelled bad and a sloshing sound came from one corner.

"What is that over there?" I asked no one in particular.

"That's our bathroom," said the girl I had stepped on. "A pail."

I wrinkled my nose. All these children and one pail for a bathroom? No wonder it smelled so bad.

I crawled as far away as I could get from the stinky pail, moving slowly and being careful not to hurt any of the children who were crammed in my way. When I got to the other side of the car, there was a thin seam of light framing a panel in the siding. It was a door. I pounded and screamed with all my might. The children who were propped up against it scooted to the side.

"It won't do you any good," said a boy's voice. "We've already tried to open it."

I looked over to him in the dim light and saw a silhouette of wild hair. There was a trickle of dark on his cheek. Was he bleeding?

Using the ridges in the siding to help me balance in a standing position, I felt a long lever across the door. I pushed it down hard. It moved and sprang back up but the door didn't open.

"It's locked from the outside," a girl's voice said.

I pounded on it again with my fists. Nothing happened.

The wild-haired boy looked up at me and said, "Even if it did open, what would you do then? Fall out onto the train tracks in the middle of nowhere?"

I slid back down and sat beside him, wrapping my arms

around my knees and staring at my feet. Was Larissa in a cattle car like this, going somewhere else? How would I find her? What was happening to me?

❖ ❖ ❖

In the dark monotony, we children exchanged names with those who sat closest to us. The wild-haired boy was Luka Barukovich from Kyiv. Sitting beside him was Zenia Chornij, also from Kyiv. The girl I had stepped on was Marika Steshyn, from Babin, not far from my village of Verenchanka. The thin seam of light around the door frame was my only marker of time. It dimmed, then darkened. I slept.

In that space between day and nightmare my body swayed with the *chug-chug-chug* of the boxcar. One child chanted prayers in a voice hoarse from crying. Gradually, the seam around the door got light again.

Daytime stretched out in endless minutes. I was hungry, thirsty, hot. Weren't we all?

A second night passed. Would we all die in this cattle car?

A loud screech and we came to a halt. The door slid open. I would have fallen out had I not grabbed onto Marika, who was curled in fitful sleep on my lap. The sudden daylight hurt my eyes and the whoosh of cold filled my lungs with what felt like a thousand tiny pins.

I propped myself up and squinted, trying to make sense of what I saw outside the cattle car. A young Nazi soldier, his face a rash of pimples, pointed a rifle at Luka. I opened my mouth to scream but no sound came out. My mouth and throat were like sawdust.

Behind the soldier stood some sort of train depot or

maybe a town. I couldn't tell for sure. There were wooden buildings that were mostly still standing, and sad looking people milling about. The only signs I could see were written in German.

A high-pitched whizzing sound was followed by a boom. In the distance, a puff of smoke. Bombs.

"Stay in there, Russian swine," screamed the boy soldier in German, jabbing his rifle menacingly.

Why was he calling us Russian, and why were we now pigs? I didn't dare ask.

He turned and motioned to someone we could not see. A door opened on one of the buildings and a hollow-cheeked woman in rags appeared behind him. Balanced on her shoulders was a long stick with a sloshing pail attached to either end. She paused beside him, awaiting further instructions.

He flicked his hand impatiently at her, indicating that she should set the pails inside our car.

"Be useful or they will kill you," she whispered to us urgently in Ukrainian, lifting one pail into our car and pushing it in against our legs. It was filled with water.

"No talking," shouted the soldier. Why did he have to shout?

He aimed his rifle at the woman.

Her fearful eyes darted to him. She lifted up the second bucket and Luka grabbed the handle. We all pushed back so there was room to set it on the floor. This one was filled with a grey watery sludge.

The door clanged shut and we were engulfed in darkness once again. The train jolted, then picked up speed.

I moved on my hands and knees over to the sludgy pail and sniffed — a dank smell that reminded me of the rotting vegetable scraps Mama would use to fertilize our garden when we still had a home. In other circumstances, the smell might have turned my stomach, but it had been so long since any food had passed my lips that my stomach rumbled in anticipation. I dipped one finger in. Lukewarm. I tasted it. "This is some sort of soup."

There were no spoons or bowls so we took turns crawling over to the pail and carefully scooping out a bit of the muck with cupped hands. In the handful that was mine, I could feel a chunk of turnip with my tongue, but otherwise it was mostly water. I chewed the turnip slowly and swallowed it down, the wet mush feeling like a balm on my dry throat.

My eyes were getting used to the dimness of our car, so I watched as the others lined up and swallowed down their meagre share of soup. Marika didn't get in line. She didn't even sit up. I crawled over to her and placed my hand on her forehead. It was cool — too cool — to the touch.

"Food, Marika. You've got to eat." I gently shook her shoulder. Her eyes opened slightly, and I thought for a minute that she looked at me, but they quickly fluttered shut.

I got back to the pail of watery turnip soup, nudging my way to the front of the line. "Marika needs something to eat."

The children closest to the pail made room for me and I scooped up as much of the solid bits as I could with my hands. It wasn't easy getting back, with the rail car swaying, the darkness and the other children. But each time I nearly fell, one of the others would steady me.

Luka and Zenia propped Marika up between them. I

knelt in front of her and held my cupped hands to her face. Her nose wrinkled. Perhaps her dreams were more pleasant than the smell of these vile bits of turnip. Her eyes opened and she looked down.

"Eat."

She cupped her fingers over mine and drew my hands to her mouth. She swallowed a piece of soggy turnip and choked.

"Slowly."

She held my hands close to her mouth as if she were afraid I wouldn't give her any more, but she carefully chewed every bit of turnip and swallowed it down. She licked my fingers, then pushed my hands away and slumped back into Zenia, exhausted.

There was barely any soup left for Luka, the last in line. We reversed the order for the water, so at least Luka got a few good swallows.

With the little bit of food in my stomach and water to wet my lips, I felt stronger. "I wonder what that woman meant, 'Be useful or they'll kill you'?"

"We're too young to be of much use to the Nazis," said Luka. "And useless people are killed."

The words were like a stone on my heart. If I was too young to be useful, what about Larissa? What could she do to prove herself useful? How could I save her? First I would have to figure out a way to save myself.

"What work could I possibly do?" I asked.

"Figure out a skill," said Luka. "And say you're older."

"How do you know about this?"

Luka sighed. "This isn't the first time I've been caught by the Nazis."

Chapter Two

Cross-stitch

A skill.

All Mama had to do was look at a dress and she could make the pattern for it. Tato was like that too, but with leather-work. They could make anything with a needle, awl and thread.

Once the Soviets invaded, Mama hummed lullabies under her breath and taught me cross-stitch on potato sacks. "Remember, Lida," she would say. "You can make beauty anywhere."

I looked around the cattle car. Was there any beauty here?

I began to sing Mama's favourite lullaby:

Kolyson'ko, kolyson'ko
Kolyshy nam dytynonku

Luka's voice answered:

A *shchob spalo, ne plakalo*
A *shchob roslo, ne bolilo*

9

Luka knew my lullaby? I would sing it with Larissa, but never before had I sung it with another child. I had always thought it was our family's personal song. I joined in, my face wet with tears:

Ni holowka, ni vse tilo.

Luka ran his work-hardened fingers gently through Marika's hair. He looked up at me and we sang the lullaby again. Others joined in, and by the third time we sang it, almost all of the children in the car were singing. I may have temporarily lost Larissa, but in Luka and the others here, I had found sisters and brothers of the heart.

My eyes were still wet with tears, but somehow singing together made the pain more bearable. We sang the lullaby over and over. Mama was right. Beauty could be made anywhere. We sang for hours until, one by one, each of us fell hoarse.

Marika's head rested on Luka's shoulder, her eyes closed in sleep. I was tired, but awake. Luka's eyes were fixed on something in the distance.

"What are you thinking about?" I whispered.

"Being locked in here reminds me of when I was taken to the first work camp."

"You escaped?"

He looked at me with eyes that seemed far older than he was. Slowly, he nodded.

"What happened?"

"I was sent with a work unit to dig ditches close to the Front, but we were hit with Soviet fire. The officer in charge was injured and so were some of the prisoners. We all scattered. I got to a village and a widow hid me. Said I reminded her of her grandson. But the Front kept moving closer. I had only been there a few days when I woke up at dawn to the ground shaking. Through the cottage window, we could see Soviet tanks lined up on one side of the street and Nazi tanks along the other. The village was in the middle of the battlefield. The widow's house was blasted to rubble with us inside. We tried to make a run for it but it was impossible."

"You were caught by the Nazis again?"

He nodded.

"What happened to the widow?"

"Dead. They thought I would be useful, but not her."

I felt tears well up in my eyes at the thought of the woman who had tried to protect Luka. My own grandmother would have done the same thing. I grabbed one of Luka's work-worn hands and gave it a gentle squeeze. "I am so sorry."

His grip tightened over my hand in response.

I felt awful about the things that Luka had had to go through, and his story left me with more questions than answers. I knew how bad it felt to be caught once, but twice? And where was his family? Maybe in time he would share that with me as well.

We sat together in silence, each wrapped in our own sadness but thankful to not be alone.

I drifted to sleep with the rhythm of a lullaby rocking me. I dreamed that Larissa was curled asleep on my lap, my arms wrapped around her. I dreamed that Mama and Tato were still alive. I held my hand up to my neck and felt the thin leather necklace that held my metal cross. It was the only thing I still had from my family.

✤ ✤ ✤

The days and nights blended from one to another until I lost count of them. One time the train shuddered to a stop, but the doors stayed closed. Would they leave us here, in this locked stinking car, until we died? Another time it stopped and the door screeched open. I gulped in the fresh sweet air for that brief moment that it took for them to shove in another batch of soup and a pail of water. How long had it been since they'd fed us last? I couldn't be sure but it felt like many days. We were all so weak that we fell into a sort of stupor.

I dreamed of the times after Mama and Tato were taken. Larissa and I going to live with our grandmother. The three of us stitching out bits of happiness however we could. I knew in my heart that Baba would not have survived that night the soldiers came and snatched me and my sister from her bed. Larissa was all I had left. But where was she now? How could I find her and make sure she was safe?

I sat up with a sudden jolt.

Had I slept for hours, or days? Time mixed together in the grey stink of the cattle car.

My scalp felt alive with a squirming itch. I ran my fingers through my hair and could feel tiny twisty things writhing on my scalp. I snatched one with my fingertips and pulled it out, nearly losing a bit of hair in the process. A bug. I crushed it with my fingernails, then snatched another and another, but the squirming continued.

Around me, children roused, and as they did, they whimpered. Like me, they grabbed at their hair and clothing and tried to shake out the bugs.

"It won't do any good." Luka was in his usual spot, propped up against the panel door, Marika asleep beside him. "With all of us crammed in here for so many days and no place to wash, we're a breeding ground for body lice."

I shuddered. For each bug I squished, a hundred would escape. Could I find beauty in this situation? I crawled over to sit beside Marika.

Her eyes fluttered open. "I don't feel well," she said. She tried to sit up but was engulfed in a fit of coughing.

I tried to help her up but she flopped back down. I gently placed my hand on her forehead. The last time I had felt her, she'd been too cool, but now she was burning. Her pale face had an angry red splotch on each cheek. I looked at Luka and was about to say something, but he shook his head. I think he realized how sick she was but didn't want to say it out loud. I took her hands in mine and stroked them gently, singing our lullaby in a low voice. Other children joined in. Untold hours passed.

❖ ❖ ❖

The train shuddered to a stop. Luka grabbed Marika by her armpits and dragged her away from the door just as it yawned open. A gust of icy air whooshed in and the sunlight was so white that it hurt my eyes.

"You dirty swine, get out now!" a voice shouted from somewhere beyond the brightness of the day.

Why did Nazis always shout?

We cringed away from him, but I was afraid of what he might do to us if we didn't get out, so I edged to the door. I tried to shimmy down, but my legs were rubbery from sitting so long. All at once I felt a blow to my head. I fell out of the car and smacked into sharp gravel on my hands and knees. My palms and kneecaps screamed with pain but I had no time to think about that. Children tumbled out above me. I rolled away and missed being trampled by a second.

Luka grabbed me by the hand. "Get up now." I looked up and squinted. Marika was in his arms.

"I can't," I said. "I'm hurt."

"You can't afford to be hurt."

Luka practically wrenched my arm out of its socket, he pulled so hard. I swallowed back the pain and stumbled to my feet, scraping them on the gravel. My eyes were getting used to the bright light. Several men brandishing short rubber clubs lined the children up at the opening of what looked like a modern fortress made of bricks and wood. The entrance was in the middle of a two-storey wooden building. It looked like an upside down U, protected with a fancy metal-and-wire gate. Above the entrance was a small house with windows. Maybe a lookout?

The Germans with billy clubs wore plain clothing but they each had a bandage on one arm with the word *Wachmann* printed on it. I knew that word. Police.

What a sorry lot we were: covered in rags, dirty, hungry, stinky and squirming with lice. We straggled inside and the gate clanged shut behind us. We stood in a cluster, fearful of what would happen next. I could hear the distant sound of sirens and the *whizz-boom* of bombs.

"Clothes off here," said a policeman.

He was making the girls undress in front of the boys? My face burned with shame.

"Take Marika," whispered Luka. He draped one of her arms around my neck and I wrapped my arm about her waist. I could feel her try to stand, but she was very weak.

We girls moved in a cluster to the back of the line. Luka turned to me one more time. His mouth opened but I couldn't hear what he said above the sound of the weeping and groaning.

A policeman struck him on the ear with his club. "Didn't you hear me?" he screamed. "Undress now."

Luka said something to the boys. They all turned their backs to us and began to undress.

"Look away from the boys," I told the other girls. "These police may make us undress in public, but we don't have to be shamed."

All at once a club crashed down on my head. "No talking."

Zenia was beside me. She quickly took off her rags and threw them into the pile, then held Marika for me as I took off my nightgown and tried not to think of my humiliation. I slipped the leather necklace with the cross off my neck but I couldn't bear to leave it with the piles of clothing. I clasped it in my fist and hoped that no one would notice. Zenia helped me undress Marika and between the two of us we kept her moving along the line.

"Go to the barber over there," shouted one of the policemen.

The barber was a bored looking man with a pot belly and the stub of a cigarette dangling from the corner of his mouth. Marika barely opened her eyes as her hair was shaved off. When it was my turn, he scraped a straight razor over my head in a series of deft strokes. I watched as clumps of my hair fell on top of the pyramid of bug-infested locks that had already collected. "Next," he said, dismissing me. I shivered as the cold air hit my scalp.

After the haircuts, we were herded into a large concrete building. The door whooshed shut behind us.

✤ ✤ ✤

Metal spigots on the ceiling opened up, and we were sprayed with some sort of liquid that stung the scrapes on my hands and knees. My lungs burned. I tried to hold my breath, but I could feel the burning in my eyes and on my lips.

After we were thoroughly soaked in the chemical, a door opened up and we fled into a second compartment. This one was a heavenly shower with plenty of glorious hot water. I let it course over my lice-scabbed scalp and down my shoulders, rinsing off the stinky chemical. Hundreds of black squiggling bugs swirled down into the drains on the floor.

The shower was over all too soon. We were herded out, soaking wet, into the wintry bright air. I slipped my cross back on, then shivered as I picked through the mound of clothing, looking for the ragged flannel nightgown that I had worn since my capture.

"Quickly," shouted a policeman. "Grab something now or go without." He smacked one of the slower girls on her shoulder with his club.

I couldn't find my nightgown so I grabbed a dress. It was damp and filthy and encrusted with lice, but at least the bugs seemed dead. I wasn't so concerned about whether I wore my own nightgown or someone else's dress, as long as I could cover myself quickly.

I shivered in the chilly air as I pulled the damp dress over my head. Marika was too weak to put her clothing on so I draped a large shirt over her shoulders and Zenia helped me get her into a skirt.

Marika had been captured wearing a good pair of sturdy shoes but I could not find them in the pile. I frantically searched through the clothing, but they were gone.

"Who took Marika's shoes?" I said to no one in particular.

A billy club smashed down on my spine. "Hurry," shouted a policeman.

We girls were then led barefoot to an open area within the fortress-like complex, Marika hobbling between me and Zenia. Marika hadn't said a word since we'd gotten out of the cattle car and her lips were blue with cold. We were ordered to stand at attention.

I kept my arms around Marika and so did Zenia, but even with our combined body heat we trembled. We were freezing, wet and frightened. I looked around, trying to get my bearings. What would they do to us here? The open area seemed to be in the centre of the complex. There was a series of long buildings along either side. Some were made of brick but most were wooden and looked fairly new. The entire complex was enclosed in a high wooden fence topped with barbed wire. High guard stations had been built into the fence at regular intervals, each containing a menacing Nazi soldier, his rifle casually pointed in our direction. Were we that dangerous?

Just then, we heard a high whine. I looked up. A formation of American fighter airplanes with stars on their side. We all instinctively flattened to the ground. The planes flew past us, not slowing down. In the distance I heard the familiar *whizz-boom* as the bombs landed.

Before Larissa and I had been captured, I had overheard adults talking about how the Americans were now dropping bombs on German factories during the day while the British bombed the cities at night. I hoped that this complex wouldn't become a target.

Before the Nazis took us, I had been glad when I heard about the bombings in Germany. I wanted the Allies to win. Baba said that if Britain and Canada and America beat Hitler, they would then fight Stalin and give us back our freedom.

A crisply uniformed officer with glossy leather boots and a long whip came out of one of the buildings, a German shepherd at his heels. He walked over to where we lay.

"Get up."

His quiet voice was more terrifying than the shouts of the policemen. I stumbled to my feet, pulling Marika up with me.

"Take your arms off that girl."

"I cannot do that because — "

The whip snapped. I felt a jolt of pain on my cheek, a warm trickle of blood on my face. The shock of pain loosened my grip on Marika and she slumped back to the cold ground. The officer towered over her. "Stand up."

Marika lay still.

He paced slowly in front of us, hands and whip held behind his back and the German shepherd a few steps behind him. The officer paused, examining each of us in turn, his disdain for us clear in his scowl.

He motioned with his hand and a policeman approached. "Get rid of that one." He pointed to Marika, then left, his dog following close behind. The man picked up Marika and carried her away.

What would they do to her? I tried to run after the policeman, but Zenia gripped my elbow. I tried to pull loose but her grip was firm. My knees buckled and I would have fallen to the ground, but she held me upright.

"Quickly," shouted a different policeman, brandishing his club. He herded us into one of the barracks.

The room was dank and dim and smelled of bleaching powder. It was an oblong room with three tiers of wooden bunks on one side and two tiers on the other. I counted: thirty-six in all. As my eyes adjusted to the darkness I could see that there was a small wooden table by the door and a bare light bulb hanging from the ceiling by a wire in the middle of the room. I walked over to it and pulled a long string that was attached to it. The bulb didn't give off much light, but I could see the room more clearly. I noticed a small electric heater up against the back wall so I walked over and touched it. Stone cold. I felt all over until I found a switch at the back. I flicked it on, then held my hands in front of it for a few moments. A faint warmth billowed out — not nearly enough to heat the entire room. Most of the bunks had a mattress folded in half, positioned at the end of the bunk. Stacked on top of each mattress was a bare pillow, two coarse grey blankets and one stiff yellow bedsheet. The bunks closest to the heater looked taken — the mattresses lying flat and the beds made.

The bottom bunk close to the door seemed not to be claimed, so I sat down on the wooden edge, exhausted, cold and hungry, but mostly in shock. So much had happened in such a short time. What was this place they had taken us to? It was better than the cattle car — at least it was clean — but it seemed that we were in some sort of prison. What had I done wrong?

Some of the girls were flipping open their mattresses and making their beds. Others sat silently on the bare wood of their bunks like me. Some were weeping. Others looked frightened. I felt like a big weight had been placed on my shoulders. I had to find my sister. Larissa would be beside herself with fear by now. But I had to get out of this place first. How was that possible when we were surrounded by a barbed-wire fence and guards? Was there any way I could get word to her? I could not let myself get sad or overwhelmed. I had to stay strong. The most important thing was to stay alive and healthy so I could find my sister and get her to safety.

I flipped my mattress down onto the bunk and was surprised at its dull thud. I ran my palm over the surface of the ticking, trying to determine what the mattress was stuffed with. At home our beds were filled with goose down. I remembered that last night before the Nazis came. Before Larissa and I were stolen away. We had snuggled up together under our grandmother's thick goose-down quilt. Baba had sung a lullaby as we closed our eyes and drifted off to sleep. That was my last happy memory. I wanted to hold it in my heart forever.

This mattress was stiff and nearly rock solid. I picked up the pillow. It was stuffed with the same mysterious filling. I held it to my face and breathed in deep, then nearly choked. It smelled like an unswept barn.

"It's stuffed with old dirty straw," said Zenia, who was busy making her own bed.

Did Germans sleep on straw? I had always thought they were cleaner than that. But they kept calling us swine. I guess they really believed it, even giving us the bedding of pigs.

I picked up the one yellow sheet and held it to my face. It was coarse and scratchy and smelled like bleaching powder, but at least it seemed clean. I unfolded the sheet and drew it over the mattress and the pillow together and tucked it in as snug as I could. I would do anything to keep my body away from that straw. The last thing I needed was another batch of lice.

The electric heater hummed away but no heat reached me. I lay down on the bunk, pulled the covers over top of me and curled up into a ball, hoping for some warmth, but the blankets were so stiff and thin that I kept on shivering. As I lay there, worrying thoughts tumbled through my mind. What would become of me? What would they do to Marika? Where had they taken Luka? I could only hope that wherever Larissa was, it was better than this.

I felt a gentle hand on my back and turned around. Zenia. We had barely talked on the train and now she was being so kind to me.

"Who else will help us if we don't help each other?" she said. It was as if she had read my mind. "Besides, if it wasn't for you, I don't think I could have survived the train ride."

Her comment puzzled me.

"You were the one who got us to sing."

My eyes filled with tears. We were human after all, and we could comfort each other, but Zenia, Luka and Marika were the only ones from the cattle car that I knew anything about. "What I'd really like to do," I said, "is find out a bit about all of us here."

"Good idea," said Zenia, smiling. "I'll start." She went back to her own bunk and lay down. "Hello, everyone, my name is Zenia Chornij. I'm fourteen, and I'm from Kyiv."

A dark-eyebrowed girl in the bunk above her said, "I am Tatiana Shevchenko, and I'm from the Kyiv region too. From Bucha."

From the bunk by my feet, a voice said, "I'm from Lychanka. We were almost neighbours."

I sat up and leaned over so I could see the owner of the voice. With her shaven head, pale eyes and blond eyebrows, the girl looked almost colourless. She wore a dark woollen school dress and filthy white stockings. "What's your name?" I asked.

"Kataryna Pich."

"How old are you?"

"Eleven."

"I am eight," I said.

There were murmurs in the room. "I've heard they don't like the young ones here," said Kataryna.

A frail looking girl from the top bunk across from mine said, "I'm from the Chernivets'ka region. I'm eight years old too. My name is Olesia Serediuk." She sat up in her bunk and peered down at Kataryna. "Who says they don't like the young ones?"

"I've heard whispers," Kataryna answered.

Some of the girls murmured in agreement, but others disagreed.

"My name is Ivanka Mychailenko," said a girl with a mole on her cheek, who had claimed the bed closest to the heater. "I'm thirteen, from just outside of Kyiv. I also heard that it is much better to be older."

The introductions and arguments went on for quite a while. Most girls were either from the Kyiv region or from my own Chernivets'ka region. The girls from Kyiv were mostly older and had been captured either right off the street or in school by regular Nazi soldiers. The ones from my area had been mostly targeted by the Brown Sisters — the Gestapo women — just as Larissa and I had. Those younger ones whose bunks were close to mine were named Olesia, Daria and Katya. Olesia seemed to be on her own, but Daria and Katya had chosen bunks side by side.

"Are you sisters?" I asked them.

Daria shook her head. "But we knew each other from church."

By the time we finished with the introductions, I realized that I wasn't the only one who had been separated from a sister or brother or parents. We listened to the constant thunder of bombs in the distance as each of us was wrapped in our own personal pain.

Olesia in particular seemed so small and alone sitting cross-legged on her bed. Her face glistened with tears. Katya slipped off her own bunk and stepped over to Olesia's. Sitting on the edge, Katya reached her hand out to dry a tear from Olesia's cheek. "We are all sad, but let's try to watch out for one another," she murmured.

"Lida, can we sing?" said Zenia, her voice cracking with emotion. "I know that we are all sad and afraid."

I took a deep breath and swallowed back my tears. I had never felt so empty in my life, but I knew in my heart that she was right. Every girl here was feeling as bad as me.

Singing would surely help. Zenia went back to her own bunk and I lay down on mine. What did it matter how many bugs were in the straw? I would have to get used to it no matter what. I closed my eyes and willed away the sound of bombs and the image of my horrible surroundings. I thought of Larissa.

In a voice strong and clear, I began to sing new words to a familiar melody:

When I was a child I had a sister dear . . .
Kataryna answered with a tremulous voice:
When I was a child I had parents who loved me . . .
Ivanka responded with:
I am still a child but I have no one left to love me . . .
Zenia's clear sweet voice sang:
You have us, dear child, and we love you . . .

Little Olesia gasped in sadness at the words, but she added her own line, as did another child and another.

My terrible surroundings disappeared and I remembered a time of happiness — with Larissa. I remembered a time before Tato was arrested by the Soviets. Before Mama was taken by the Nazis. We had a lilac tree behind our house. The last spring we were together, I had lifted Larissa onto my shoulders and stood under that tree. She had reached up and picked a single sprig. We put it on our kitchen table for Mama.

How I loved the scent of those lilac blossoms. I breathed in deeply, willing myself to smell their delicate scent. For a moment it almost worked, but only for a moment. Instead of blossoms, all I could smell was rotting straw, bleaching powder and misery.

Chapter Three

Russian Soup

The door opened with a loud shriek. I bolted upright, memories scattering.

It wasn't an officer or a policeman, but a tired looking woman with frizzy hair bound up in a bun. She wore a faded dress with an apron over top. She clapped her hands and said, in that kind of clipped Ukrainian that the Germans who lived in my country used, "Quickly, children. You must come with me."

She sounded almost kind.

She had us line up in front of two policemen who sat outside one of the administrative buildings at a wooden table. When it was my turn, one of them took my hand and pressed the tips of my fingers onto a black pad and then firmly pressed my inky fingers onto a small white form. He waved the form in the air to dry the ink, then handed it to his fellow officer, whose fountain pen was poised.

"Name?" he asked, without looking up.

"Lida Ferezuk." I watched him write down my name using German letters instead of Cyrillic.

"Date of birth?"

"March fourteenth," I said.

He looked up briefly and said, "Happy birthday."

Today was March 14? So I was now nine years old. The last days and weeks had been a blur of sadness. My birthday was the last thing on my mind.

"Year?" he asked.

"Nineteen . . . " And then I hesitated. If I told the truth, what might they do to me? Would they consider a nine-year-old to be useless? I couldn't take the chance. "Nineteen thirty."

"Are you sure you're thirteen?" He looked up, clearly not convinced.

"Yes, officer."

He wrote it in, then looked at me, his mouth curved into a near smile. "Consider that your birthday present."

"What is your country of origin?" he asked.

"Ukraine."

"No such place."

I watched as he filled the space with *Occupied Eastern Territory* — a term I hated.

"Place of birth?"

"Verenchanka," I said, then added, "Chernivets'ka region, Bukovyna, Ukraine."

He slashed a line through several spots without asking anything. In the part where it specified nationality, he left it blank.

"Can you put that I'm Ukrainian in that spot?"

"No such thing," he said. "You're finished."

Kataryna Pich was the next person in line. I was curious to hear how old she would make herself, so I paused.

"February sixth, nineteen twenty-nine," she told him.

She had made herself fourteen instead of eleven! The officer didn't question her, but wrote down the year and date with studious boredom.

"Go to the *Kantine*," he said to her as he finished. He looked up at me and said, "You, no dawdling."

Kataryna stepped away from the table and the two of us stood in the next spiralling lineup. We had both heard each other lie about our ages. I squeezed her hand and her pale blue eyes met mine. "I hope we guessed right," she said.

The moment we entered the *Kantine*, I could smell the food despite being so far down in the lineup. Meat in gravy, onions, even vanilla? How long had it been since we'd last eaten? A day? Two? Long enough that my stomach had forgotten how to growl. Even before the war, food was not plentiful. It hardly seemed in keeping with the way the Nazis had treated us so far. Perhaps my nose was playing tricks on me.

Conversations of people lined up with me buzzed in the whispers of many languages. The Russian I could understand by listening carefully. Some of the words were the same as Ukrainian, but others were not. The German I could understand. A German family had lived on our street, but the Soviets had taken them away. I caught wisps of unfamiliar tongues as well.

I looked around at all the people. Some wore rags faded to dirt grey and others were clothed in tattered party dresses, nightgowns, school uniforms. It all depended on what they were wearing when they were captured. Some wore mismatched shoes or wooden clogs. Most were barefoot. I looked down at my own bare feet, now blue with cold. Wooden clogs would be good. Some of the prisoners wore badges on their clothing — mostly square blue-and-white badges with OST in the middle, but there were some diamond-shaped P badges in purple and yellow. There were no yellow stars like my friend Sarah had had to wear.

I craned my neck to see if I could find Luka and the boys from our cattle car, but I couldn't. When we were almost at the front of the line, the warden pointed to a stack of bowls, tin cups and spoons. "Each of you shall take one bowl, cup and spoon. After you've eaten, you will clean them and take them to your sleeping quarters."

I clutched my bowl, cup and spoon to my chest and stepped forward in hungry anticipation. The wonderful scent of cooking had revived my appetite. Our warden stood at the front of the serving window, her arms crossed and a look of boredom on her face.

When I finally got up to the front, I smiled at the cook, who stood sweating beside four open vats of soup, three clustered together and one set apart. Each vat had a tidy label painted on the front: *German, Aryan, Polish.* The one set apart from the others was labelled *Russian.*

My mouth filled with saliva as the cook ladled out a bowlful from the German pot, with its chunks of meat, potatoes and carrots floating in greasy thick broth. A person in front of me held out her bowl. After filling it, the cook reached to the table behind him for a dish of vanilla pudding! He gave that to the prisoner as well. I could hardly believe my eyes.

I waited for the people in front of me to be served.

When it was finally my turn, I held up my bowl and said, "I would love some German soup, please."

The cook barely glanced at me. Instead, he looked over to the warden and raised his eyebrows.

"Russian," she said.

"I'm not Russian, I'm Ukrainian."

The warden frowned at me. "Do you see a sign here that says Ukrainian? You're from the east. You're Russian."

The cook stepped over to the lone Russian pot and slopped some of its contents into my bowl, using a separate ladle. I looked down at the murky brown mess and my eyes filled with tears.

"Could I at least have some pudding?"

"We don't waste precious food on sub-humans," she said. "Go sit now."

What did she mean by sub-human?

I balanced the bowl and made my way through the maze of jostling people. I found a spot to sit at a long wooden table. I sniffed the soup. A faint rotten smell. I dipped my spoon in and swirled it, trying to figure out what it was made from. The skin of a turnip rose to the surface. I stirred again. A small white curly thing — a worm? Bile rose at the back of my throat. I pushed the bowl away.

"You'd better eat it," said a voice in German with an accent I didn't recognize.

Sitting across the table from me was a girl not much older than I was. She didn't wear a badge but she looked like a prisoner. Her black hair had grown out a few centimetres from the shaving she must have received upon arrival. It stuck out like bristles on a hairbrush. How long had she been here? Her eyes looked bruised with exhaustion, but her mouth curved into a faint smile. She dipped a spoon into her own soup with relish and pulled out a small chunk of meat.

I was outraged. "Why do you get meat and I don't?"

"They don't consider you a valuable human," said the girl.

"All humans are equal."

"The Nazis consider you sub-human," said the girl, gesturing with her spoon. "Just look around. There are people from many countries that have been brought here to do labour for the Germans. Some are political prisoners — like me. I was caught distributing anti-Nazi leaflets. Others were captured — like you. The German police and soldiers get to eat the best food because they are the most valuable humans. They even get vanilla pudding for dessert." She dipped her spoon back into her soup and placed a chunk of potato on her tongue. She chewed slowly, as if savouring the taste. "But I'm Hungarian and they consider me a valuable human because my government is allied with the Nazis."

"What do they consider Ukrainians?"

She took another spoonful of soup and swallowed it with a satisfied look. "No such thing. Don't you mean Russian? Or maybe Polish?" Her eyes lit up with excitement. "If you get the choice, tell them you're Polish. They get better food than the Russians."

"I don't think I get to choose."

"Too bad." She shoved a chunk of meat that glistened with fat into her mouth. She chewed another mouthful of her tasty smelling soup and her eyes met mine. "You'd better eat up," she said. "Or another Russian will come and steal it from you. All you Russians are thieves."

I looked down at my bowl of goop and dipped my spoon back into it. A worm? So what? It was as close to meat as I would be getting for a while. It was important to keep up my strength so I could get out of this place and find Larissa. I filled my spoon as full as I could and shoved it into my mouth, trying not to gag at the awful taste. I kept my eyes locked on the Hungarian girl's face as I chewed.

I licked my bowl clean, making sure not to waste the merest morsel of turnip. All too soon, our warden stood at the door of the *Kantine*. She clapped her hands sharply and said, "Barracks Seven, we leave now."

We were scattered at different tables but we all stood and went with her.

Chapter Four

Zenia

"Luka!"

He stood with some other prisoners in a lineup at the entrance to the men's bathroom — a wooden building that looked like a small barracks. I was in the line for the women's bathroom, which was beside it. Luka's head turned when he heard his name and his eyes met mine briefly, but his face stayed a mask of sadness. He stepped into the bathroom, and a few minutes later, came out. He walked past my lineup and when he got to me, he stopped.

"Stay out of the hospital," he whispered.

"Move!" a policeman shouted at him.

A billy club glanced off Luka's back. His eyes widened in pain but he did not cry out. The policeman grabbed Luka's arm and shoved him back into line.

What a brave friend Luka was. How had he managed to find out about the hospital? And how kind of him to take such a risk to let me know. It surprised me that the hospital was somehow bad. If I'd had time to think about it, I would have assumed it would be the best place to be . . . Except . . . Larissa! It was a hospital-like place where she and I had been separated. Was she still there? Maybe in danger? Now I worried about her even more.

I was pulled out of my thoughts by a revolting smell that made my nose wrinkle. I looked up — my turn next for the bathroom.

Zenia was a little behind me in line, so she held onto my eating utensils. When I stepped inside, my bare feet landed in something wet. It was all I could do to keep from gagging. My eyes adjusted to the dimness and I saw six wooden doors. A woman came out from behind one and held the door open for me. Inside was a rough slat of wood with a hole in it. I held my breath and did what I had to as quickly as I could, trying to imagine that I was in my own outhouse at home, which had always been clean and fresh.

I nearly ran out of there, gulping in the fresh wintry air to clear my lungs of the stink.

"That bad?" Zenia asked, seeing the look on my face.

I nodded. She handed me my eating utensils and also her own. It was her turn for the bathroom.

Little Olesia was lined up behind Katya and Daria outside another small wooden barracks, so I stepped in behind her. Her freshly shaved head was covered with bright red bug bites. There was one long scratch from the barber's blade under her left ear. Her feet were bare too, but she wore a skirt and a wool sweater — a much more substantial outfit than my own thin dress. She turned to me and sighed. "This place is awful."

Just then the line moved forward and we stepped inside the building. It turned out to be our wash house. On the floor was a big metal basin that reminded me of a pig trough. Fifteen faucets came out of a water pipe that ran at waist height along either side of the trough. I turned on one of the taps and cold water gushed out.

"Is there any soap?" I asked Olesia.

"Only this." She handed me a pail of white powder.

I shook some out onto my dampened hands, but realized right away that it wasn't soap. It was a harsh bleaching powder that made my hands burn. I quickly rinsed most of it away, but used a small bit to clean my feet. With no shoes or socks and the cold dirty ground, I did not want to get them infected. The bleach stung as I massaged it into the tiny cuts on the soles of my feet, but it felt good to be a little bit cleaner.

I rinsed my hands off in plain cold water, then used a bit of the bleaching powder to clean my dishes and Zenia's. There was nothing to dry myself or the dishes with, so again, when I got outside, the wintry air hit me.

The warden was waiting for us outside our sleeping barracks. She handed Zenia a stack of rough cloth patches, thread and needles. "You must wear these Ostarbeiter patches on your clothing at all times," she said. "That way, everyone will know that you are Eastern Workers. Anyone found not wearing the OST badge will be shot."

She ticked off each of our names on a clipboard as we entered our sleeping quarters. "Tomorrow is Monday. You will rise at four-thirty," she said sternly. "When you hear the whistle, get up. No dawdling."

Zenia gave each of us one of the patches. Now that I

looked more closely, I could see that they were made of a coarse white material that had been stamped with striped bands of dark blue ink. In the centre were the initials OST.

Olesia sewed her patch on hastily, then climbed into her bunk. Zenia finished next. I watched as each girl did the job quickly and fell into an exhausted sleep. I was also tired, but to have a needle with thread made my fingers tingle with memory. Yes, the OST badge was ugly, and what it symbolized was even worse, but Mama always told me to find beauty where I could. Instead of stitching sloppily just to get it over with, I savoured every stitch, taking care to make each one perfectly. Even as it grew dark, my fingers became my eyes and a delicate pattern revealed itself. Thinking of Mama brought forth the image of those lilac blossoms. Hardly realizing it, my fingers created simple petal-like stitches — beauty to surround the ugly OST. If Mama were here, she too would have been able to make even prison clothing beautiful.

A beam of moonlight shone through a wooden window slat and illuminated Zenia's pale face, wet with silent tears. I crept over to her bunk and huddled close. There was nothing I could say that would comfort her. I knew that we were all feeling lonely and frightened, but all of the other girls had managed to sleep.

I put my hand on her shoulder. "Is there something I can do to make you feel better?" I whispered.

She shook her head. "Nothing can help. I am all alone in the world."

I was hungry and cold and frightened, but I could hold on as long as there was a chance that Larissa lived.

"But how can you know for sure?" I asked her. "There is always hope."

Zenia pulled me close. I could feel her hot breath on my ear. "I'm Jewish."

I felt like a rock had been thrown at my heart. None of the prisoners had yellow stars.

It was a miracle that Zenia herself had managed to survive for this long. I remembered when the Nazis came to our town. At first we were relieved that it was not the Soviets, for we thought no one could be as bad as them. My father had been one of the thousands they killed just days before the Nazi invasion.

My friend Sarah and her parents were just as hopeful as we had been. Germans were civilized, weren't they? But then they took the Jews and shot them. Mama had tried to hide Sarah and her parents, so they shot my mama too. Larissa and I heard the shots from our hiding place in the attic.

There was only one difference between the Nazis and the Soviets: the Soviets killed by the cover of night, but the Nazis killed in full daylight.

If the Nazis found out that Zenia was Jewish, would she be killed on the spot? My hand went up to my neck and I caressed my crucifix. I had been powerless to save my friend Sarah, but could I help Zenia? My simple cross was not just jewellery and it was not only a symbol of my beliefs. It was all that I had left of my parents. But it also showed that I wasn't Jewish. Should I give this to Zenia? Could I bear to part with it? But Zenia had so much more to lose. I had no choice. I had to give it to her.

I took it off, held it to my lips and kissed it goodbye.

Then I pressed it into Zenia's palm. "Wear this."

Her eyes filled with tears but she said nothing. I tried to understand what she must be thinking — that wearing the cross was like denying her family, denying the religion her parents had died for. But she had to blend in. And she needed a reason to live.

"If you don't live, who will tell your story when the war is over?" I asked her.

Her eyes met mine. She looked back down at the crucifix and her eyebrows knitted in thought. Another minute passed. Then she sighed and her eyes met mine. "You're right." She slipped the leather necklace that held my crucifix over her head. "Thank you."

Chapter Five

Work

Somehow I slept. In the background of my dreams I could hear the incessant *bang-bang-bang-boom* of British airplanes targeting a nearby city with a blanket of bombs. They were so close I could feel my bunk tremble.

Memories of scents and tastes crowded out the bombs — lilac blossoms, vanilla pudding, wormy turnip soup. A flash of Larissa: fear in her eyes and her arms outstretched. "Lida, please don't leave me!" I tried to grab her but she was just a dream. All too soon the morning whistle shrilled and I tumbled out of my bunk.

We were given half an hour to get up, tidy our beds, use the bathroom and wash in the cold water. The warden herded us to the *Kantine*, where we were each given a triangle of black bread the size of my palm and a tinful of coloured water the cook called tea.

I sat between Zenia and Kataryna at one of the long wooden tables and pulled a chunk of bread off my ration and put it in my mouth. It had an odd woody taste, unlike any bread I had ever eaten, but I was starving so I chewed it slowly, washing it down with sips of the brown liquid.

Zenia bit off a piece of her bread and chewed thoughtfully. "This is made of sawdust."

When we were finished, we took our bowls, cups and spoons with us and the warden herded us back out into the open area.

"Stand at attention," she said.

We weren't the only prisoners. I recognized a person here and there who had been served a bowl of Russian slop the night before. I also saw Luka in one of the rows ahead of me. He stood with the boys from our cattle car, looking as dazed and exhausted as I felt. They each had OST badges stitched onto their clothing. He turned and caught my eye for a brief moment. I nodded my head slightly. He winked, then turned back around.

The warden made us stand at attention for what seemed like an hour, but finally the door of the main building opened and that same officer from the day before stepped out. He held a stack of forms in his hands. Behind him was a man in civilian clothing. He carried a tripod and had a camera strapped around his neck.

"If I call your name, step forward." He read out names from the forms.

From our barracks he called Daria, Katya and Olesia. A few boys from our cattle car were also identified.

"You are all under twelve," he said in a firm clear voice. "You will not be required to work."

I glanced over and caught Olesia's eye. She gave me a faint smile. I think she was glad now that she had given her true age.

He looked up from his forms and studied our pathetic group. "Is there anyone under twelve that I have missed?"

I tried to make myself stand tall, hoping it made me look older. I did not want to be caught in my lie. Besides, I remembered what that woman had whispered to us as she shoved the pail of soup into our cattle car. *Be useful or they will kill you . . .*

Kataryna Pich stood not far away from me. I didn't want to look at her, but from the corner of my eye, I could see her standing in place as well. She did not step forward.

"Surely there are more of you twelve and under," he said. "We have room for at least one more."

I could barely breathe, I was so afraid he would order me to stand with the younger children. I did not move. Kataryna stayed where she was.

I heard footsteps behind me. Tatiana stepped forward. She was definitely older than twelve. "Stand over there," the officer ordered, pointing to where the photographer had set up his equipment. One by one, each child was photographed. Our warden checked off names on her clipboard after each picture was taken.

The officer walked down our rows, inspecting us one by one. He stopped in front of me. "Stand with the children and get your photograph done."

"I'm thirteen," I said in a voice that I hoped would be convincing.

"You're too small." He nudged me with his whip. "Go. You won't have to work."

I looked over to Olesia, who stood with the younger children. Her eyes met mine and it was like I could almost read her thoughts. *Tell the truth,* her eyes said. *Admit that you're younger — it's safer.*

But I could not do that. My heart told me that she was wrong. It was safer to be older, to be useful. I had to save myself if I was going to save my sister. I prayed that I was guessing right.

I met the officer's cold blue eyes, then let my gaze rest on his sharply pressed uniform. One button was just a hair looser than the rest. And there was an inch or so of frayed edge on his collar.

"You have no seamstress."

His hand went to the loose button and he frowned.

"What would you know about that?"

"The button simply needs tightening. The shirt — where it's frayed — that requires a deft hand to fix."

One eyebrow rose. His eyes seemed to focus — to notice me as an individual. They moved to the delicate stitchwork around my OST badge. The other eyebrow rose. He touched my badge.

"You did this pattern?"

"Yes."

"Well, well. A little Russian with clever hands. How unusual." The warden nodded in acknowledgment of his joke.

I held my breath.

"After you're photographed, stand over there." He pointed to his office.

The photographer snapped my picture and I walked to the door of the officer's building. I stood rigidly at attention, my eating utensils clutched in one hand at my side and my face impassive. I watched him designate a few other girls as children, and one more boy from our cattle car. The officer passed by Luka without stopping.

When he was finished his inspection, he walked over to a waiting policeman.

"Get these older ones photographed and take them to work."

Luka and the others had their faces recorded for the Nazi record keepers as well. After that, they were marched out the gate and onto an idling train.

Those who had been designated as children stood in a cluster, looking smug. The officer snapped his fingers to beckon another waiting policeman. "These go to the hospital."

The hospital? Luka had warned me about it. What would happen to Olesia and the others? My imagination swirled with a hundred deadly possibilities. How I hoped that Luka was wrong.

As the younger children were led away, Olesia turned and waved. She looked almost happy. I felt sick.

The officer walked over to me. "So you're my little seamstress?"

His mouth curled into a smile but his eyes stayed cold. What had I got myself into? He stepped past me and opened the office door. Was I to follow him? He'd given me no indication. I stood rigid, still at attention, waiting for orders.

The door closed.

It stayed closed for minutes. An hour. I kept at attention, fear growing in my belly. My hands were stiff with cold and my feet were frozen blue. The sawdust bread sat like a lump in the pit of my stomach.

The door opened. The officer's uniform was un-buttoned. His brow crinkled with an uncomprehending frown. "Aren't you my seamstress?"

"Yes, sir," I said through cold lips.

"Then get sewing."

"Yes, sir." Did he expect me to sew with no needle and thread and no clothing to fix? Was I to be a magician as well as a seamstress? That is what I felt like asking him. Instead, in as meek a voice as I could muster, I said, "Where should I do my sewing, sir?"

He walked back to his office and left the door opened, so I could see him pick up a telephone and dial. He spoke firmly to someone, then slammed the receiver back in its cradle. He closed the door and I waited some more.

A few minutes later, a thick-legged woman with a red face appeared from one of the side streets. She walked quickly towards me. "You're the girl who sews?"

I nodded.

"This way." I followed her as she retraced her steps. We reached a stone house set slightly apart from the build-ings. She pushed the door open and a huge cloud of steam billowed out, enveloping me in its warmth.

"Get in here quickly," she said. "I don't want the heat to escape."

It took my eyes a few moments to adjust to the haze. Through the steam, I could see an industrial-sized vat and what looked like mounds of white cotton sheets and tow-els being swished back and forth in hot soapy water by a huge mechanical arm.

"This is the laundry," she said. "My name is Inge and you're to help me."

"I thought I was supposed to sew."

She looked at me and smirked. "Oh, you'll do that too. Once my laundry is done. If your sewing isn't finished, you'll be in trouble and I don't care, but if the laundry isn't finished on time it will be me in trouble, and I do care about that."

I wasn't in a position to argue. I had to make myself useful to Inge — so useful that she'd want to protect me.

She put her hands on her ample hips and looked me up and down. "You'll get the laundry dirty in that getup," she said. "Take off your dress."

"But the OST badge," I said, touching it with my fingers. "I was told never to take it off."

"In here you do as I say." Inge opened a cupboard and took out a bar of soap and a fluffy white towel. "Clean yourself. Quickly."

After I had washed in gloriously hot water with real soap, Inge gave me a smock that smelled of bleaching powder. "You'll wear one of these smocks each day in the laundry," she said. "You can change back into your own disgusting outfit before you leave."

It was back-breaking work, helping Inge lift wet sheets and towels out of the water and put them through a mechanical wringer that squeezed out the excess water. We rinsed them, wrung them out again, then rinsed a second time in a fresh vat of water, then wrung them out a third time. My arms ached from holding up the heavy cloth, but I was warm right down to my toes.

When the sheets and towels were finally clean, I helped her hang them on clotheslines in an enclosed courtyard behind the laundry house. They wouldn't dry completely

— it was too cold outside for that. But while they flapped in the wind, we started on a second batch of laundry.

I was light-headed with hunger and every muscle in my body ached from the hard work. Hours had passed and I still hadn't been allowed to do a single stitch of sewing.

A whistle shrieked.

"Mealtime," said Inge. "Change into your old clothing. Come back from the *Kantine* as soon as you've finished eating."

"Yes, ma'am," I said, pulling the clean smock over my head and folding it neatly. My lice-encrusted dress felt horrible as I stepped into it.

Inge looked at me not unkindly and said, "You're a hard worker for your size."

Her words were like a balm to my soul. I was useful. Did that mean I would live? If only she would let me get some sewing done. "Thank you, ma'am," I said. I grabbed my eating utensils and scooted out the laundry-room door.

Chapter Six

Seams

It seemed much less crowded in the *Kantine* compared to breakfast. Entire tables were empty and there were only a few people in front of me at the soup lineup. I watched hungrily as the cook filled the bowls of the people in front of me — a Polish prisoner, an Aryan, then me.

The cook looked at my OST badge and set down the ladle he was using. He stepped over to the vile Russian soup and spooned some of it into my bowl with a different ladle. I looked down at my soup. It was the same as yesterday's — turnip and water, with maybe a lump or two of oats or potato. He filled my tin cup with some sort of hot dark liquid. Then, "Out of the way," he said, gesturing with the ladle. "You're holding up the line."

I looked behind me. No one was there.

I carried my bowl to an empty table and took a seat that faced the entrance. I was hoping that Luka might come in, or maybe Zenia or Kataryna.

"May I sit here?"

I looked behind me. It was the Hungarian girl. If she was so disdainful of me being sub-human, why did she want to sit with me? "You don't need my permission."

She set her bowl on the table and sat opposite me.

She was wearing the kind of uniform that those nurses who separated me from Larissa wore, but this girl's was grey and frayed from many washings. Even from across the table, I could smell the meat in her soup. It made my stomach lurch with hunger. Why in this whole empty place had she chosen to sit with me? I looked around the room. I was the only one here who was younger like she was. I took a spoonful of my soup and swallowed it down.

When she took a spoonful of her own soup, I noticed what looked like a spray of fresh blood on her cuff. Where did she work?

"You didn't take the train," she said. "That's good."

"Don't they come back here for their meals?"

She shook her head. "It would waste too much time. Workers are dropped off at different spots along the route. Some move rocks, others work in factories. They eat their soup wherever they work."

Surely they wouldn't make Kataryna move rocks? And could Luka or Zenia operate factory equipment? What about the rest of the children? I hoped and prayed that each of them would be able to prove themselves useful.

"How long have you been here?" I asked, my eyes concentrating on my soup.

"Six months."

I looked up at her in surprise. She didn't seem as smug as she had the day before. Her eyes — still looking bruised and tired — brimmed with tears. What was her job?

"My name is Juli," she said. "What's yours?"

"Lida."

"That's a pretty name." She dragged the back of her hand across her face, drying the tears.

"Yours is pretty too."

A faint smile formed on her lips. "Sorry for being so mean yesterday."

I nodded, swallowing down a spoonful of soup. "How long do we have before the whistle goes?"

"Lunch is sixty minutes." She filled her spoon with vegetables and a chunk of meat. As it hovered in front of her mouth, she looked at me guiltily. "I would share this with you, but they would shoot me."

I nodded. It was kind of her to say. I watched as she shoved the spoon into her mouth and chewed on meat, potatoes and vegetables. How I longed to reach over and take a spoonful from her bowl.

"Where are you working?" Juli asked.

"The laundry."

"One of the better places."

"What about you?"

"The hospital." She shuddered, as if she were holding the weight of the world.

"There were some children from our group who were taken to the hospital this morning," I said. "Daria, Tatiana, Olesia and Katya — did you happen to see them?"

Juli looked at me with blank eyes. She didn't answer, but instead methodically dipped her spoon into her soup again, then placed it in her mouth.

I set my spoon down and glared at her. "I asked you a question."

She chewed her spoonful of soup and sighed. In a voice barely above a whisper she said, "Do not ask about this here."

I looked around and couldn't see anyone who was interested in our conversation. What was it that Juli couldn't talk about?

"Is it as terrible as I've heard?"

She didn't answer, but from the pleading look in her eyes, I knew that I should drop the subject.

"Eat," she said. "This is the only break you'll have until we finish at six. You still need to visit the outhouse, wash your bowl, take it back to your barracks and get back to the laundry."

I looked around and saw that others were quickly slurping. I shovelled in the rest of my soup and swallowed, feeling some vile chunks of turnip going down whole. I held the bowl up to my lips and let the last brown drops drain into my mouth. Juli did the same with her bowl. I gulped down the dark liquid in my cup. It tasted different from the morning's tea, but was awful in its own way.

Juli hastily stood up and left, as if she wanted to get away from me as quickly as she could.

When I got back to the laundry, Inge was sitting at a table with a piece of waxed paper opened in front of her. On it were the remains of a devoured sandwich — a couple of crusts, a bit of mustard. She was biting into a second sandwich made of fresh light-rye bread and thick slices of roast pork. The aroma made my knees weak. How I longed to eat those remaining crusts.

"Go change," she said, a bit of pork falling from the end of her sandwich as she bit into it. "Then start taking the laundry off the line out back. I'll meet you there in a minute."

The sheets were stiff in the wintry air and they were awkward for someone as little as me to handle all by myself, but I was determined to prove that I was useful. By the time Inge had finished her sandwich, I had taken down and folded four of the sheets. She didn't praise me, but I could tell by her smug silence that she was pleased with how much work I could save her.

My hands and feet were sore with cold by the time we got the rest of the sheets folded and brought inside.

"These need ironing," she said. I followed her into a room beyond the washing area. This one had a tall steam press that reminded me of a coffin with a levered lid. Was she expecting me to operate it? I would need a ladder to get to the levers. Along one wall was an oversized table, which I assumed was for folding the ironed sheets. Maybe I could pull that over to the ironing press and stand on it?

"While I'm ironing, you shall mend," said Inge.

Thank goodness.

I took the stiff top sheet off the pile and spread it out on the folding table. I ran my fingertip along the frayed outer edge. "Is it the seams that you want me to mend? These are all going to fall apart if they're not re-sewn."

"That's what you're here for." Inge plugged in the huge ironing contraption to let it heat up and then stepped over to my side. "It would be more sensible to do the seams with a sewing machine," she said. "But they're all in use making new uniforms for the war."

"May I begin now?" I asked her. "It takes time to do this by hand."

Inge got a wicker sewing kit out of the cupboard —
small spools of thread in different colours and weights, a
black velvet needle cushion holding several sizes of needles, and a small thread snipper. The kit looked too
domestic for an army.

Without wasting any time, I pulled a chair over to the
big table and sat down to my work. I threaded the nar-
rowest needle from the cushion and knotted the end of
my long white thread. I double-folded the frayed edge of
the first bedsheet and deftly worked in a narrow chevron
stitch, using the edge of my thumbnail as a ruler.

Inge stood over me and watched. "You're good at that.
Tidy and artful."

I nodded my head slightly in acknowledgment of her
praise and kept on stitching. If I was going to prove my
worth to the officer, I needed to have an impressive
amount of perfect work done.

The steam press had heated enough for Inge to use, so
she left me to my mending and began to tackle the folded
mound of damp sheets. As she worked, she hummed a
melody that must have been German. I didn't recognize
it. I stayed silent. I needed to concentrate on making fault-
less chevron seams.

When I was finished my first entire sheet, I stood up
and stretched the kinks out of my back. Inge took the
sheet from me and examined each stitch.

"This is fine work," she said. "It will look like new once
this sheet has been ironed."

She put it through the giant press and I was pleased
with the results. My stitches were just as I had wanted
them — tidy and even like a machine had made them,

but with a pattern that no machine could do.

"I guess I can trust you with this, then." She brought me the roll-call officer's uniform jacket and shirt and set it on the table in front of me.

The uniform smelled faintly of tobacco and sweat. I threaded a thicker needle with sturdy grey thread and fixed the loose brass button on the uniform. That part was easy. Fixing the frayed collar without having the mend show was trickier, but I managed.

Inge snatched it from me when I had finished, held it up to the light and carefully inspected it. "This will do," she said. And she almost smiled.

"You can mend one of the ironed sheets," she went on. "I'll run the edges through the press a second time to tidy them once you're finished."

The ironed sheets were smooth and warm and easier to work with. By the time the 6 p.m. whistle blew, I had managed to hem two entire sheets and a good portion of a third. I had pricked myself a few times, but hadn't got a single drop of blood on any of the cotton. My hands and back ached from the concentration, but I was pleased with myself. There were worse places than this warm clean laundry.

I had wanted to stay longer to finish the third sheet. I was so fearful that the officer would think I had worked too slowly.

"I will tell him you're a good worker when I take back his uniform." Inge tapped her foot, waiting for me to finish. "Now go. I'll see you tomorrow."

Chapter Seven

Bloodstains

The cold air caught at my throat as I stepped out of the steamy warmth of the laundry building. My feet hit a patch of ice on the gravel surface of the walkway and I nearly lost my balance. I hurried into the girls' bathroom and was surprised to see that it was empty.

When I stepped into the wash house to clean my hands, I startled Juli, who was alone there, frantically scrubbing. She had sprinkled some of the bleaching powder onto the bloodstains on her cuff and now all that was left was a wet pink patch. I noticed for the first time how swollen and chapped her hands were. How many times since she got here had she needed to wash away blood?

She saw me staring at her hands, and I guess she must have realized that I saw the pink stain too. She rinsed off the bleaching powder and held her hands behind her back.

I wanted to ask her about the blood on her cuff, but sensed that this wasn't the time.

"Where is everyone?" I asked instead.

"The train is not back yet," she said. "By the time every-one gets picked up and dropped off, it will be another half hour or so."

What a long day it was for those people who were work-ing away from the camp. It was gruelling for me and I had one of the best places to work.

I washed my hands in the cold water, using just a tiny bit of the bleaching powder. I needed to stay clean because I didn't want to get those bugs back again. The powder stung the tips of my fingers, especially where I'd poked myself with the needle.

Juli stood there expectantly, as if she were waiting for something or someone. "How did you make out with the sewing?" she asked.

"I think I did fine," I told her. "Inge seemed pleased."

Juli's shoulders relaxed. "I am relieved to hear that."

I stepped to the door of the wash house and stuck my head out. No one else was waiting to get in. We were alone. I came back in and regarded Juli.

"Please," I said. "Have you seen the children they took to the hospital this morning?"

Her eyes filled with tears and she sat down on the edge of the giant metal wash trough. "I did see them," she said. "But you must put them out of your mind."

I could feel the frustration building inside me. Why wouldn't she tell me what they were up to? Surely she realized that not knowing was worse than the most horri-ble reality. "Please, Juli," I said. "I must know."

She breathed in a deep shuddering breath and stared at the cement floor. "Not all of the children suffer the same fate," she said. "So I'm not sure what happens to them all."

"But what have you seen?"

She touched the pink stain on her cuff. "Blood," she said. "They remove it."

My mind went blank. Then I managed, "I don't understand what you mean."

"They put a needle in the child's arm and drain out blood into bottles. A lot of blood."

I tried to imagine a needle going into Olesia's arm. She would be so frightened. And what about Larissa? Had the nurses at that other place taken her blood as well? The thought of it made me ill.

"What would they do that for?"

"They send it to the Nazi soldiers who are fighting on the Front. If the soldiers are injured, they lose blood. They get an infusion of children's blood to make up what they've lost."

The room swirled. Did the Nazis see us as nothing more than spare parts for their war machine? My knees buckled and I crashed to the floor.

In an instant Juli was down on the floor beside me. She cradled my head on her lap. I could feel a hot tear splash onto my forehead.

"It's terrible," she said. "I know it is. But I do everything I can to make them comfortable. Mostly they die in their sleep, and in war, that is not such a bad death."

The thought of little Olesia being bled to death was horrifying. She had been so hopeful that her choice had been right. I thought of the other young girls — Daria and Katya. And of Tatiana, who had chosen to pretend she was younger. I thought of our introductions in Barracks 7. I was just getting to know them and now they were gone.

I also felt guilt. If I had stepped forward and been truthful about my age, maybe the officer would have told Tatiana to step back. Did I have blood on my hands too? I held my fingertips close to my face and looked at the red pinpricks. I deserved these hurts. I was a horrible person.

I curled into a ball on the hard cold floor and wept. I wept for the children who had died, and I wept for all of us still living. I thought about my dear Larissa and prayed that this was not her fate. I wept for my parents and all of the other parents who had been killed by the Soviets or the Nazis. The despair enveloped me and I choked through my tears.

Juli's hand felt warm on my back. "I'm glad that you lied about your age," she whispered. "Otherwise it could have been your blood on my clothes."

The words were like a slap in the face. I stopped crying. Juli helped me sit up.

"What do you do with the children?"

She shuddered, but managed to look me in the eye. "I clean up after the doctor has taken the blood." She let out a huge gasping sob and collapsed into my arms. "When the doctor and nurses go on their break, I try my best to comfort the children. I sing to them and give them water. I wish I could do more."

The two of us clung to each other and wept.

Chapter Eight

Grey Ghosts

Suddenly the door to the wash house burst open. Zenia, Kataryna and Anya stepped in. They nearly tripped over me and Juli.

"That's not a very good place to take a nap."

I opened my mouth to respond, but when I turned towards Zenia, I got the shock of my life. The person standing in front of me looked like a ghost. Zenia was covered in a powdery soot from head to toe, her eerily familiar smile seemed suspended in air.

Juli helped me to my feet. My head still swirled with a combination of hunger, fear and horror, and Zenia's appearance did nothing to make me feel better.

"What happened to you?" I asked.

"This is metal dust," she said, trying to brush a bit of it off her forearm. "I'm working on small machinery, using a power sander to smooth out the seams on newly welded pipes." She walked over to the wash trough and turned on a tap, then splashed water and bleaching powder on her face and arms. Rivulets of the dust whirled down the drain. "There's no window or fan in the room and this dust fills the air like fog, it's so thick." Slowly the Zenia I knew emerged from behind the ghost-like apparition.

I helped her wash the dust from the back of her neck and the top of her scalp. It was encrusted all over the cross I had given her too. "It can't be good to breathe in all that metal dust," I said.

"I'm sure it isn't," said Zenia. "It's probably why there are no Germans in that room — " She started coughing and ended up spitting phlegm into her hand. I could see that it was laced with streaks of grey.

We were barely finished when the wash house was over-run by more workers coming back from their assignments. The smell of bleaching soap, metal powder and sweat was bringing back my dizziness, so I got out of the building as quickly as I could, gulping in the cooler air, hoping my knees wouldn't buckle again.

A long snaking lineup had formed in front of the out-houses and washing rooms. Not all of the people were children. I recognized some from the morning's assembly. About half looked like Zenia — exhausted ghosts — covered head to toe with a fine grey powder. Some had soot-blackened hands and feet. Others just looked bone-tired.

It took me a while to spot Luka. He was one of the grey ghosts. I caught up with him as he stood in the lineup for the men's wash house. "You're doing metal work?"

He nodded. "It's not the worst job."

Making her way through the crowd of slave labourers was our warden, a sour expression on her face. She clapped her hands sharply to get our attention. "No dawdling," she shouted. "If you've finished cleaning yourselves, get back to your barracks."

"Go," said Luka. "You don't want to get into trouble."

I was the first to step back into Barracks 7, exhausted and hungry and sad. I sat at the edge of my bunk and looked at the room with its straw-stuffed mattresses and scratchy blankets. Such a small and mean place for thirty-six young girls.

My eyes rested on the bunk that had so briefly been Olesia's. It seemed hard to believe that I would never see her again. I looked at the neatly made beds of Daria, Katya and Tatiana. I closed my eyes and said a silent prayer for their souls.

I stretched out onto my bed and stared at the wooden bunk above me. I barely had to reach to touch it. Did they put the adults in bunks this small? Even the workers who built these bunks must have known that no one could be comfortable in them. I bundled up my blanket and pretended it was a stuffed toy, hugging it to my chest. Where was Larissa now? If I thought hard enough about her, would she be able to read my thoughts? *Larissa, Larissa, dear sister . . . I love you . . . I'll find you . . . Stay safe . . .* I must have fallen asleep, chanting my wish for Larissa, because the next thing I knew, the barracks door creaked open. I sat up with a jolt.

The warden's silhouette was framed in the entry. "You there, on the bed," she said to me. "Show these new girls where they should sleep."

She ushered in three girls, then left. Their heads were freshly shaved and their clothing stunk of the lice chemical. Each girl's outfit had a purple P stitched on a yellow diamond-shaped patch of cloth.

Just last night, Olesia, Daria, Katya and Tatiana had slept in this room with me. We had gotten up together and eaten breakfast. It was bad enough that they were now gone. But for them to be replaced already? Were we really nothing more than pieces of machinery? I looked at these three and at first I was angry. They wore P for Polish, which meant that they'd get better food than the rest of us. That was bad enough, but to take the place of our dead friends was dreadful. I wanted Olesia and the other girls back.

But I looked at the three new girls and saw the fear in their eyes. It wasn't their fault. I wasn't the first one to sleep on my bed either. We were prisoners, after all. I swallowed back my anger and held out my hand. "My name is Lida."

A gangly girl with knobby wrists reached out and grasped it. "I'm Oksana," she said in Polish, shaking my hand vigorously. "This is my little sister, Marta." The girl beside her stepped forward and shook my hand. Although she was Oksana's younger sister, she was an inch taller. Her eyes were a startling green, made more so from their tear-reddened rims.

"I am Natalia." The other girl thrust her hand out. She was the shortest of the three, but she was sturdily built.

"Are any of you under twelve?" I asked.

"I'm fifteen," said Oksana. "Marta's fourteen."

"And I am fourteen as well," said Natalia.

"That's good," I said, leading them over to the beds that were now empty. "Don't say you're younger. You'll be safer if you're over twelve."

"We know that," said Oksana. "This isn't our first camp."

I told her to have Daria's bed and gave Marta the bed that had been Katya's. Tatiana's bed would do for Natalia. I kept Olesia's bed empty. Would it stay empty? Not likely. But I couldn't bear to see a replacement girl sleep in it quite yet.

The new girls were almost settled in when Zenia walked through the door. Soon after, a stream of girls who had worked outside the camp came in as well.

Zenia got undressed, dropping her filthy blouse and skirt onto the floor. She pulled her bed apart and wrapped herself in her scratchy blanket. "We're taking turns washing our clothing, Lida," she said. "If you wash mine now, I'll wash yours tomorrow."

She bundled up her clothing from the floor and handed it to me.

I took the bundle from her. Natalia offered to wash some clothing too, so she and Ivanka, one of the older girls from the Kyiv area, stepped out the door with me. I was surprised to see that it was dark.

"We have to hurry," said Ivanka. "Lights out at seven and it's six-thirty already."

When we got to the wash house it was empty except for one stick-thin woman who looked to be older than my mother. She had the same idea as us and was busily scrubbing a bundle of colourless rags with a rock. She looked up when she heard us come in. "You must be new here," she said. "I'm Mary."

We introduced ourselves to her and got down on our knees in front of the trough.

Mary had plugged the drain with a bit of wood and had filled the trough with water, but there were carcasses of dead lice mixed in a bleachy scum of sweat and dirt on the surface of the water.

"Do you mind if I freshen the water?" I asked her.

"I was just about to. Go ahead."

We watched as the scum swirled down the drain and then sprinkled our own laundry with a liberal dose of bleaching powder. Mary handed me her rock. "Better to scrub with this than your fingers," she said.

I thanked her and took the rock from her hands. It was amazing all the stuff that came out of Zenia's clothing, yet when I was finished, it looked almost as dirty as when I started. It was the best I could do.

"How long have you been here, Mary?" I asked.

"I think it's been eight months," she replied. "You lose track in here after a while."

"Where are you from?"

"Irpin, outside of Kyiv."

"How were you taken?"

"Soldiers raided our secret school," she said. "They took all of us."

I knew that schools had been disbanded when the Nazis invaded, so secret schools had popped up every-where. A dangerous act of resistance. "Were you the teacher?" I asked.

A wave of surprise, then understanding, passed over Mary's face. "I guess I've aged," she said. "I was seventeen when they captured me. I'm — "

A whistle blew and Mary stood up.

"Lights out in ten minutes," she said. "You'd better

hurry." She wrung out the excess water from her laundry and walked out the door.

Natalia, Ivanka and I walked quickly in the darkness back to Barracks 7, holding our dripping bundles of clothing in front of us so we didn't get wet, but I shivered anyway in the March night air with just a thin dress on and bare feet. All around us, other prisoners were rushing about, trying to get things done before lights out.

"How did you end up here?" I asked Natalia.

"The three of us were at a different camp. Some of the prisoners revolted, demanding better food. Some were shot. Others were sent to different places. The three of us worked in the kitchens and we were not part of the revolt, so we got off easy compared to others."

"Where are you from originally?" asked Ivanka.

"I am from Lviv," said Natalia. "The two girls with me, Marta and Oksana, they're from Drohobych."

"Are you Polish or Ukrainian?" I asked.

"I'm Polish. Marta and Oksana are Ukrainian."

"At least you Poles will all get better food than we do," said Ivanka.

When we got back to Barracks 7, I helped Zenia drape her blouse and skirt at the end of her row of bunks. Would they dry by morning? Hard to know. All we had to warm the room with was the body heat of thirty-five frightened girls and one small stove, whose warmth seemed to stretch no farther than six inches.

I lay back down on my own bunk, pulled the covers over me and tried to stop shivering. Would I ever get used to walking on the wintry ground barefoot? But I was grateful that at least I was working inside in a warm place every

day. Yes, every muscle in my body ached, and yes I was tired, but I was alive.

I thought of Olesia, Daria, Katya and Tatiana. I was grateful that I had been spared, but it made me feel guilty too. They were so young, yet no one had helped them stay alive. Would someone help Larissa? I prayed that she had met up with people who could look out for her, who would treat her well until I could find her. I closed my eyes and tried to sleep, but hunger gnawed at my belly and thoughts of Larissa haunted my dreams.

With a sinking feeling, I realized I must have slept through supper. "Can someone do me a favour tomorrow?" I said to no one in particular. "Please wake me up so I don't miss supper."

Stiff blankets rustled and there were a few suppressed chuckles.

"It's not funny," I said. "I'm starving."

"Silly girl," said Zenia. "None of us got supper."

Her words slapped me in the face. A triangle of sawdust bread and a bowl of watery turnip soup and that was all for the entire day? No wonder Mary had aged so quickly in a matter of months.

"When I get out of here, the first thing I'm going to do is eat a piece of fresh homemade bread slathered with butter and dripping with honey." It was Natalia who said that.

"Don't talk about food," said Zenia.

"I won't," said Ivanka. "How can we talk about fresh bread, or butter and honey when we're all so hungry? I wouldn't want to talk about the beautiful tortes my mother would make, or soup made with wild mushrooms my brother picked in his secret spot in the woods . . . "

My stomach grumbled with hunger. "Can't we talk about something else?"

But try as we might, the conversation kept on coming back to food.

I fell into sleep, dreaming of my grandmother's poppy seed cookies.

✤ ✤ ✤

The blast of the early morning whistle and the next day began. Then the next, the next and the next. They all knitted together with sadness, hunger and cold. We laboured through March and April and into May.

Each day was much like that first Monday. We would get up in the dark and work until it was practically dark again. Twelve hours was usual, although there were a few who toiled longer. Every few days, more labourers would arrive by train, yet it seemed that the camp always had room for more. On Saturdays we finished at noon, and Sunday, glorious Sunday, we usually had off.

The higher-class prisoners who didn't wear the OST badge were allowed to use the train and go into town on Saturday afternoons and Sundays. A few did housekeeping for German civilians and would be fed as payment. Oksana and Marta used the privilege of their P badge to go into town and sell items that we girls in Barracks 7 made in our off-hours — sculptures made of discarded wood with a sharpened spoon as a carving tool, or small bits of embroidery made with thread and fabric I stole from the laundry. The two girls would stand in the streets, hawking our items. It was a dangerous thing to do and money was worthless in the camp, but they could barter for a piece of lard or a chunk of horsemeat, and these little bits kept the rest of us in Barracks 7 alive.

In the summer months, farmers would wait outside the camp on Saturday afternoons with their trucks. They would take a few lucky souls with them to work in their fields, and since there was no roll call on Sunday morning, those leaving on Saturday afternoon often wouldn't come back until Sunday night. Juli was one who would go, and so would Natalia. How I longed to tear off my OST badge and go with them. But it wasn't just the OST badge, it was proper papers, and those I didn't have.

For Juli, it was the same farmer who picked her up each Saturday. She told me that Herr Klein and his wife despised Hitler and that they were kind and generous. They insisted that she eat at the table with them and their young daughter and she was served as much food as if she were family. Juli told me that they had two sons in the German army, both fighting on the Eastern Front. That sent chills down my spine. The Eastern Front was Ukraine!

Juli knew that if she was found smuggling food in, she could be shot, but she took the chance when she could. Once she smuggled in a thick piece of real bread made with rye flour. I wept for joy.

Natalia didn't go with the same farmer each week. Most Saturdays she was paid in food and she would share whenever she could. Once she smuggled back a handful of real coffee beans. Each of us in Barracks 7 got at least one. I got two. The burst of flavour when I chewed the beans was glorious, but then all night I tossed sleeplessly, wondering and worrying about Larissa. Had she been taken to a camp like this? How could she possibly prove herself useful? I had worked myself up into such a worried state by the morning whistle that I vowed never to eat another coffee bean, no matter how delicious they were.

For brief snatched moments on the weekends, Luka and I would sit together behind the girls' wash house and talk about life before the war. His father had been a pharmacist, but his store had been confiscated by the communists. In secret, Mr. Barukovich had continued to help the sick, and he began teaching Luka the art of mixing drugs.

"But our neighbour informed on him," said Luka. "Tato was paraded through the streets as an 'enemy of the people.' Some of those he had secretly helped came out to watch. Not that I blame them — what else could they do? He was sentenced to ten years in Siberia."

"Where is he now?" I asked.

"Still there, as far as I know. . . . Or dead."

"Do you have any other family?"

Luka nodded slowly. "My mother," he said. "She might be alive, somewhere in Germany. She was taken as a slave labourer before I was."

"I want this war to end," I told him. "Then you can find your parents and I can find my sister."

Luka squeezed my hand. "Until that time, let's watch out for each other. You are like the sister I never had."

His words warmed my soul.

Often, by the time the weekend came, I was so tired that all I could do was sleep. It was a way of briefly escaping the hunger and the cold and sadness. But every once in a while on a Sunday morning from ten until eleven, the Nazis would let us have a recital, and no matter how bone-weary I felt, I always went to listen. It was astonishing how many wonderful singers were at our camp. Some people made crude musical instruments out of pieces of wood and string and metal. I would sit there and listen with tears running down my face and think of my mother's truth: that beauty could be found anywhere.

Bare feet and a thin dress is not much to wear in a Bavarian winter, so the warmth of August made me thankful. On the coldest days when we first arrived, I had considered tearing up one of my blankets and making it into warmer clothing, but our warden told us that we would only be issued those two blankets for the whole time we were here, and that could be years. We were not allowed to use them for clothing, and we were to guard them against theft.

As Inge got used to me she no longer made me spend so much time doing the laundry. I got to sew most of the day, and even though the work needed to be done quickly and well, I was grateful for the clean job and thankful that I was proving myself indispensable. And as the days progressed, it wasn't just bedding and towels that I worked on. Inge brought in her personal items too, so I darned knitted socks, mended flannel nighties and hemmed silken slips. For the officers, I mended woollen greatcoats and fur-lined hats. As the various kinds of fabric slipped through my fingers, I longed to have some of it for me and my friends. Those socks would feel so good on my feet, and how wonderful it would be to have a clean dress to wear.

One sticky September day, I got up my nerve and asked Inge if I could wash my own dress in the laundry.

Scrubbing it with a stone and using the bleaching powder had worn it quite thin and I was afraid that it would eventually fall apart. What would I do then?

Her eyes widened in surprise at my request. "If I could let you, I would," she said. "But how could I let the lice and dirt from your clothing mix in with the laundry for Germans?"

"But the soap here would wash it all away," I said. "Who would know the difference?"

She shook her head slowly. "If Officer Schmidt saw you in an outfit that was suspiciously clean, he would immediately know what I had allowed. I cannot risk it."

Chapter Nine

The Hospital

One fateful afternoon in October, as I sat in the laundry with sewing on my lap, I heard a *whizz-boom-crash* that was so close, the ground rocked back and forth. Had a bomb hit the work camp? Inge turned off her giant steam press and ran outside. I followed her as she trotted between the buildings until she got to the open area. A few policemen had already gathered. Juli was there as well, standing rigid in her white smock, her eyes searching in the direction of town.

She pointed. "That's where it hit."

I shaded my eyes with one hand and squinted so I could see farther — curls of smoke rising a mile or so beyond our barbed-wire enclosure.

Officer Schmidt stepped out of the administrative building and walked to where we stood. "It's the metalworks factory," he said to the policemen. "I was just notified."

Luka and Zenia worked at the metalworks factory! My heart pounded in fear for them.

Officer Schmidt turned to Inge. "Other buildings in town have been hit as well, so they're scrambling to provide first aid. Everyone who can be spared needs to get to the entrance. They'll be bringing the injured labourers back to the camp for treatment and many will need to be carried to the hospital."

Inge nodded. "I'll round up the kitchen workers and stretchers." She turned to me and said, "Lida, you're too small to carry any of the injured. Go to the hospital now with that worker — " she pointed at Juli " — and help her make up the extra beds." Then she dashed off to the kitchens.

"Come on," said Juli, grabbing my hand.

The hospital was the last place on earth that I wanted to be, but I had no choice. When we got there, Juli held the door open and pulled me in. The first thing I noticed was the strong smell of bleaching powder and I found this comforting. At least it was clean. The entryway was a small room with wooden benches along the wall and a glassed-in reception area beside a second door. Juli nodded to the white-uniformed woman behind the glass and then opened the second door, which revealed a series of rooms on either side of a long wide corridor. I followed her down the painted concrete floors of the hallway, glancing fearfully into each room as we passed. Everything looked so normal. Each room held eight or so wooden beds with straw mattresses similar to the bunks in our barracks, only these were neatly made up with good white cotton sheets, and instead of being stacked in tiers, they were all on the floor. The first room was empty, but in the second, two of the hospital beds were occupied. The man and woman had a uniformity about them — both were gaunt and motionless — looking more like corpses than patients. No nurse or doctor was in attendance.

"Are those people forced labourers?" I whispered to Juli.

She frowned and put a finger to her lips.

Who would hear us? But just then, a couple of nurses and a man in a white coat stepped out of a room at the end of the hallway. The doctor took no notice of us, but carefully noted something on his clipboard as he slowly walked with the nurses down the hallway towards us.

He looked up as we drew closer to the group. "I see they gave you a girl to help you make up the other rooms."

"Yes, Herr Doctor," said Juli, nodding to him in deference.

"Do it quickly, then. The train with the injured is on its way." He and the nurses continued down the hallway and went out through the door.

Juli took out a stack of clean sheets from the linen cupboard and handed them to me. I followed her into one of the next rooms. I didn't think anyone would be able to hear us as we worked so I tried to ask Juli again about the patients, keeping my voice low just in case.

"They're Germans," she whispered. "They're being slowly starved to death."

I could barely hide my shock. "Why would the Nazis starve Germans?"

"They are no longer useful," said Juli. "The woman was a warden. She has advanced cancer, and the man has a head injury. He used to be one of the police."

I continued to make the beds in silence, but my mind

tumbled with conflicting thoughts and fears. A hospital was supposed to be a place of healing, but it was at a hospital that my sister was taken from me. At this hospital some patients had been treated for injuries, but healthy children had been killed for their blood. Now here were Nazis using hospitals to kill even Germans they considered not useful. It seemed that everyone was a piece of a big machine, and if you stopped working, you were thrown out. What part of the machine was my sister being used for? She was so much younger than I. How useful could she possibly be? A dozen terrifying scenarios fluttered through my imagination. Could Larissa survive?

I made a final snug corner on the sheet of the last bed and put my hands on my hips, regarding all of the newly made-up beds. Would this room be used for healing or killing?

I heard the chugging of the train as it approached. "Let's go," said Juli.

As I walked beside her to meet the train, all I could think of was that hospital. I didn't envy Juli, having to work there every day. It had to be horrible for her to witness things she had no way of stopping. The image of those two dying Germans was burned into my mind. If the doctors and nurses were supposed to make them die, why such a long process as starving them? My memory flashed back to when I was little and the Nazis had taken all the Jews and shot them in broad daylight. They shot my mother that way as well. It seemed that just as there were different soups, there were different ways of being killed, depending on your nationality.

The cook and other kitchen workers had gathered at

the front of the gate with stretchers. The doctor was talking rapidly to the workers, gesturing with his hands. Close by stood the nurses, waiting for their orders. These women reminded me of the nurses who had separated me from Larissa. Were they here to assist the injured, or were they more interested in sorting through them? I thought of them as big white birds, circling, looking for scraps of meat.

The train pulled up, and one by one, survivors limped out of the train cars, gashes of red on their scalps and arms. Some held onto each other for support, trying to look less injured than they were. The nurses dispersed among the wounded, assisting those on the spot who just needed first aid — dispensing a bandage here and quick stitches there. Those more seriously injured were seen by the doctor.

Just then Zenia got off the train. She was cradling her left arm. Her dress hung in shreds and she was splattered with blood, but she was walking. I wanted to help her but Juli held me back. "Don't call attention to yourself," she said. "It will not help your friend."

The doctor walked up to Zenia and did a quick examination of her arm. "Surface scratches only," he said. "You're lucky." He called a nurse over to dress Zenia's cuts and went on to someone else. The nurse roughly swabbed the deep scrapes on Zenia's arm with a disinfectant, then bound it up. "You can recuperate in your barracks," she said, turning to another worker.

Zenia's face was white and covered with a sheen of sweat. I think she was probably relieved that her injuries were minor, but she still looked like she was in pain. She walked to where Juli and I stood. I guess she wanted to prove that she was still useful. I put my arm around her. "Let me help you to our barracks," I said.

"No," she said, trembling. "I'd like to stand here and assist if necessary."

The next train car pulled up and the doors opened. Two labourers carried out a third by the arms and legs. I stood on tiptoes and was horrified to see the one being carried was Luka.

"Stretcher," said the doctor, waving his hand to the kitchen workers. The cook and his assistant set a stretcher on the ground and the two OST workers gingerly lowered Luka onto it. From where I stood, I could see that the entire top portion of one leg was covered in blood. His arms and face were also spattered, but seemed uninjured.

"Luka!" I cried.

His eyes fluttered open and he looked around for me, but Juli held my arm so tightly that I couldn't run to him. The doctor examined him quickly. "To the hospital," he said.

My heart sank. Would he be treated or killed? I turned my face to Juli but she refused to look at me.

More slaves were taken to the hospital. "I have to go help them," said Juli, her voice cracking. She left Zenia and I standing there.

I wrapped my arm around Zenia's waist. "No," she said, pushing me away. "I must walk on my own."

Once we were in the privacy of our barracks, she collapsed onto her bunk in a quivering mound of pain. What could I possibly do to help her? I grabbed my own blankets and covered her up, then I got my tin cup and ran outside to get some water. I helped her drink a little bit, and held her until she fell asleep.

✢ ✢ ✢

Before the morning whistle, I was woken by Zenia's hand on my shoulder. "Look," she said, her eyes filled with tears. She had wrapped herself in one of the blankets. She held out what was left of her dress. Her tossing and turning in the night had caused even more shredding to her already threadbare dress. It was unrepairable and basically unwearable. I tore off the bottom strip of my own tattered dress and stitched that in place to make the top of hers decent.

At roll call, those who were wounded were given alternate duties. Zenia was sent to work in the kitchen.

I went back to the laundry, worried sick about Zenia. She wasn't as physically injured as many were, but I knew that the bombing had shattered her. I was especially worried about Luka. I counted the hours until lunch when I could ask Juli about him.

Inge acted as if the bombing had never happened. In fact, in the morning she looked happier than I had ever seen her.

"I've received a package from my husband," she said, her eyes shining like a child's on St. Nicholas Day.

She went into her office room and came back with an armful of extraordinary finery: a butter-coloured chiffon blouse with intricate lace at the bodice, a set of six monogrammed ladies' handkerchiefs and a heavy black fur coat. The items seemed so out of keeping with life as I knew it at the camp, and it made me wonder what Inge did when she left here each day after the six o'clock whistle.

None of the items needed mending, as far as I could tell.

"They're beautiful." I placed a fingertip on the lace.

"Aren't they, though?" said Inge. "My husband is fighting in France, and he sends me the most wonderful things."

I knew all about the Nazi soldiers and how they stole. In my hometown of Verenchanka, we had no fur coats worthy of stealing, or chiffon blouses or other high-class ladies' items. We were poor people, but our places of worship had fine old things in them — the very same reason that soldiers had bashed down the doors to Sarah's synagogue. I'd seen one soldier grab the ornate silver menorah that must have been over a century old. Sarah was nearly hysterical when he tossed the menorah onto the top of a wheelbarrow full of plundered antique samovars and oil paintings. When they were finished robbing the synagogue, they ransacked our blue wooden church, taking the icon of the Madonna, blackened with age. It wasn't made of anything fancy, but our church had been built in 1798. Mama said the icon was older than the church. Even now, the memory of that awful time made my chest tight with despair. I breathed in deeply and tried to set aside my thoughts. For Inge's benefit, I pasted on a smile. "How generous of your husband," I said. "He must love you very much."

She smiled at that. "He's always been such a good provider."

I picked up the blouse and examined all of the stitch work carefully. The lace was handmade. The entire blouse was in perfect condition. A faint scent of rosewater tickled my nostrils. Was that the preferred perfume of the lady who used to own this blouse?

"What would you like me to do with this?"

"The name," she said, turning the blouse inside out and showing me a satin label that had been securely stitched below the piping at the nape. Delicate embroidered letters in a fancy script spelled out *Mme V. Fortier*. Inge's stubby finger rested on the label. "Can you remove that and embroider my name in its place?"

Who was Mme Fortier and how willingly had she given up this beautiful blouse to Inge's husband? I held the label close to my face to get a good look at the stitchery. The attention to detail for the stitch work on an invisible label was astounding. If I removed these stitches, the label itself would likely be left riddled with holes. "Why don't I remove this altogether?"

Inge's eyebrows raised. "Why, because that's easiest for you? I want the label, and I want my name on it."

She took one of the handkerchiefs from the stack and unfolded it. The same faint scent of rosewater was released. A delicate pattern of butterflies and flowers was rendered in silken French knots. In one corner were the initials *VM*.

I had no silk thread, and even if I did, I would never be able to match the colours. I would have to untie the knot work in the initials and carefully pry out the stitches one by one, making sure not to break the thread because I would have to reuse it. Was it possible? I prayed that it was.

Inge dropped the fur coat onto my lap and I was enveloped in its warm rose-scented silkiness. How I longed to fold myself into it and fall asleep for a million years. She folded the front placket open to show me the black silk lining and the inner left pocket: the same initials were embroidered there as well, in blood-red silk thread.

"These are mine now." Her bottom lip jutted out like a spoiled child. "I want my initials on all of them."

It wouldn't be easy to change the monograms, but from the look on Inge's face, I knew she wouldn't take no for an answer. "I can do it, ma'am, but it will take time."

Her broad face broke out into a smile. "I knew you could," she said. "My initials are IP. On the blouse, you can put *Frau I. Pfizer.*"

Chapter Ten

A New Dress

I don't know how I could have managed to complete my task if it hadn't been for the electric lamp Inge brought to me, and a special magnifying glass that she borrowed from somewhere. The magnifier looked like the kind that Mr. Apramian — our town jeweller — used to use when he was doing repairs. It was like a one-lens eyeglass. With it fitted over my right eye, I could see every twist and bend in each silken knot. With painstaking care, I used two sewing needles to untangle the VF from the first handkerchief. As I feared, where the stitches had been, holes remained. When I restitched IP, I tried to incorporate the old holes as best I could.

"Give me that," said Inge, snatching the jewellers' loupe from my brow. I held my breath as she examined the stitch work on my first altered handkerchief. "This is magnificent," she declared, handing the loupe back to me. "Honestly? I didn't think you could do that."

I exhaled in relief, oh so thankful that she approved. I

knew that there were still some damaged fibres that showed through, but if she didn't notice them, I wasn't going to point them out. The rest of the handkerchiefs were easier, now that I had done one, but it still took me the entire morning to complete them.

My head was pounding by the time the whistle blew for lunch. "Come back early if you can," said Inge. "There is so much work for you to do."

"Yes, ma'am," I said. I felt like slapping her.

I stood in line for my turnip soup and coloured water, craning my neck, looking for Juli. I found her at a table in the back, sitting with a pale-faced Zenia.

"Luka," I said to her urgently as soon as I sat down. "How is he?"

Juli met my eyes and smiled. "He is going to be fine," she said. "Once they washed away the blood, it turned out to be not such a bad wound. They stitched his leg. No broken bones."

I was so overwhelmed with relief that I thought I was going to cry. "Is he still in the hospital?"

Juli put a spoonful of her meat soup in her mouth and swallowed. "They're giving him injections to make sure he doesn't get an infection. He should be out in a couple of days."

My heart sank. "Injections?"

Juli shook her head. "Don't worry," she said. "He's in one of the good rooms. They are treating him."

But I did worry.

I took a spoonful of my turnip soup and swallowed down a vile lump, then turned to Zenia. Her skin was papery white and her eyes looked huge. The repair I had done on her dress was not holding up very well. One shoulder was covered by mere threads. She picked up her tin cup and sipped some of the coloured water.

"What job do they have you doing in the kitchen?" I asked.

"Peeling potatoes," she said.

My stomach grumbled at the thought of all the potatoes she must have seen. "Were you able to sneak any extra bites?

She shook her head. "The cook was watching me like a hawk. But it's better in the kitchen than in the factory." She smiled.

I smiled back at her, then caught Juli's eye.

"I need to see Luka."

Juli looked at me with alarm. "He will be out in a few days. You can see him then."

I stared down at my bowl of soup. Juli was right. It would be easiest to wait, but I had an ache in the pit of my stomach every time I thought about him. Until I saw with my own two eyes that he was fine, the ache would stay there.

"Is the medical staff at lunch?"

Juli nodded, tipping her head slightly in the direction of the far corner. "They're mostly here now."

I picked up my bowl and gulped down the rest of my soup, then stood. "See you later, Juli and Zenia." I touched my lips with my index finger and they were both silent. I could feel two pairs of eyes on my back as I walked out.

There wasn't much time left before lunch would be over, but I didn't want to draw attention to myself by hurrying. I took my bowl, cup and spoon to Barracks 7 without washing them first, then walked with what I hoped looked like nonchalance, towards the hospital. The only person I passed along the way was the warden of one of the other barracks. She hurried past me as if I didn't exist.

When I got to the hospital I pushed open the door and stepped into the main hallway. The cool medicinal air enveloped me and I was struck by the eerie quiet. I was relieved to see that the receptionist was not there. I poked my head into the first room. Each bed was filled with a sleeping Ostarbeiter. They all looked clean and bandaged. Odd that they were all asleep at the same time. Is this what the injections were for? I was about to step back into the hallway when I heard footsteps. I hid behind the door and watched as a nurse walked into the room and took the pulse of a patient, marking something down on her clipboard as she finished. My own pulse raced and I held my breath.

She checked on a few more patients, then walked out the door. I waited until she was in the next room, then darted out to the hallway and into the third room. Luka was there and like the others, he was fast asleep. I stood at his bedside, my heart pounding. Should I wake him or leave him alone? His face was too pale but he looked well cared for. I brushed my fingertips gently through his short black hair.

His eyes opened. "Lida!" he whispered, clasping my wrist with a strong grip. "What are you doing here?"

"Checking on you."

He smiled. "I'll be fine." His eyebrows knitted into a frown. "I'm glad you came. There is something I need to tell you."

He pushed himself up to a sitting position and looked around at the other hospital beds, making sure that everyone else was still asleep. He crooked his finger and I stepped in more closely.

"If we are separated," he whispered. "I will find you after the war."

I looked at him in alarm. "Do you know something?"

"Go. You cannot get caught in here."

Before he could stop me, I planted a light kiss on his forehead. "I want you out of this place."

Luka smiled. "Me too."

I stepped behind the door just as the nurse walked into the room. I waited until she was busy with a patient, then slipped out. I hurried down the hallway, but when I opened the front door, Juli was waiting there.

"Hide around the corner," she said. "Two of the nurses are on their way."

I slipped around the side of the building, waited a few minutes, then scurried back to the laundry. My heart was still pounding by the time I got there, but I couldn't stop grinning. I had seen with my own eyes that Luka was fine and I hadn't got caught doing it.

Altering the monogram on Inge's fur coat was relatively easy. The black satiny material that lined the coat seemed to smoothe back into its original weave as soon as the red stitches were removed. It was like embroidering on completely fresh cloth. It took me less than an hour. I had left the blouse until last. The label was narrow and the material itself was slippery, so it was difficult to hold onto, let alone to remove stitches from. Before I started, I sketched the ornate letters onto a piece of paper so I would remember what they looked like. Inge wanted her name to be embroidered in a similar fashion. I sketched out Inge's name in a few different styles on the paper and let Inge choose, because it was better to make mistakes on paper than on that delicate fabric.

Inge was so pleased with my work that she took the blouse from me as soon as I was finished and put it on over top her of work smock. The blouse was tight on her and I was horrified at the thought of her ripping it to shreds and then expecting me to fix it, but what could I say?

"You look beautiful," is what I decided on.

Inge grinned. She ran into her office at the back and grabbed the fur coat, slipping that over top of the blouse. She twirled around and the coat flared out, swirling in soft lushness, the scent of rosewater wisping to my nostrils.

"You are such a divine little worker," said Inge. "I would like to reward you."

She hurried back to her office. When she came back, she was no longer wearing the fur or the blouse, but in her hand was a waxed-paper package tied with a string.

"Here," she said. "As your reward, I saved you half my lunch."

My mouth filled with saliva at the thought of the delights in that package. Each day she ate two sandwiches — always thick slabs of meat between generous slices of freshly baked bread. Even through the paper, I could smell garlic, onion, caraway, beef. Against my will, my hand stretched out and caressed the paper.

"Take it. You deserve it."

I held the wrapped sandwich in both of my hands. This was the most precious gift I had ever received. How I longed to tear the package open and gobble down the sandwich.

But a sandwich would be gone in an instant. And after eating that and enjoying it, how could I go back to the turnip soup and the coloured water?

I pulled my hand away and clutched it on my lap, willing it to be still.

"Please, ma'am," I said, looking into her eyes. "This is very generous of you, but what I would really like is a new dress."

Her eyebrows knitted together in confusion. "A new dress? But you get to wear a clean smock every day." She looked down at my bare feet. "Maybe a pair of woollen socks instead?"

How wonderful it would be to have a thick pair of socks, especially with winter approaching, but how long would they last? My feet still ached constantly, especially at night. It was tempting to say yes to the socks, but if I wore socks, how would that make Zenia feel, who was nearly naked in her ripped dress? And Ivanka and Natalia and the others in my barracks? Me wearing socks was sure to make them feel worse about their own situation.

"My friend Zenia," I told her. "She was injured yesterday in the bombing. But aside from that, her dress was ruined. That's why I'd like a new dress."

Inge's eyebrows rose and a look of astonishment transformed her face. "You would give a well-earned gift away to someone else?"

I bowed my head and stared at her shoes. "Yes, ma'am, if that's allowed."

Her warm hand brushed my shoulder. "You are just

like my husband. He works hard for the luxury goods he acquires, but then he sends them to me."

She brought in a huge basket of clothing for mending and sorted through it, a look of concentration in her eyes. "I can't give you anything too fine because it will only cause problems for you. Not this, not this. Hmm, this is too good." She looked up at me. "Ideally, I'd like to give you a smock, but they're not mine to give." She continued sorting through the basket, then pulled out a flannel shirt, dark blue, with a torn sleeve. Her eyes lit up. "Stand," she said. "Let's see how long this is on you."

She held it up to my shoulders. The shirt came down practically to my ankles. But it would work for Zenia. She was taller than me.

"Ah, this is perfect," she said, handing it to me. "Are you sure you wouldn't like a pair of socks instead?"

I took the precious shirt and cradled it in my arms. It felt substantial and it smelled clean. My eyes filled with tears. Inge had not beaten me or yelled at me since I had gone to work with her, but this was the first time she had treated me with real human kindness.

"Thank you, ma'am," I said. "This shirt is perfect." I was so grateful that I felt like hugging her, but I thought better of it. "Your generosity is appreciated."

Inge smiled. "I've always prided myself on my generosity."

I kept that dark shirt beside me as I started in on the mending that had accumulated in the laundry basket. I could hardly wait until the whistle blew and I could give my gift to Zenia. She would be so surprised! The anticipation of her pleasure lifted the cloud of sadness that had hovered over me since Larissa and I had been captured by the Nazis. Most of the time I felt so powerless, and that is the worst feeling of all. But the joy of seeing Luka and being able to help Zenia made the difference between hope and despair.

When the six o'clock whistle blew, I changed into my own rags and burst out of the laundry-house door, the shirt clutched to my chest. My face and arms smashed into something solid. I fell into the dirt, landing on my hands and knees. The shirt flew out of my grip and landed in a cloud of dust.

In front of my face was a pair of black boots, shiny through a light veneer of dust. I looked up. It was the roll-call officer.

"So the little seamstress is a thief."

I snatched the shirt from the ground and stumbled to my feet. I stood at attention before him, acutely aware of my filthy dress.

"Officer, I did not steal this shirt."

"We'll see about that."

He grabbed me by the ear with such force that I thought he would pull it off. He opened up the laundry-house door and hollered, "Inge, get over here."

Drawers closed and doors opened out back. Inge walked in to the washing room, wearing her newly personalized fur coat. She looked at me quizzically, then at the officer.

"What is the problem, Officer Schmidt?"

"Did you give this girl a shirt?"

Inge put her hands on her hips and glared at the man. "I did."

He let go of my ear. I exhaled.

"You shouldn't be giving the Ostarbeiters presents, Inge."

"It's an old shirt of my husband's, too worn to be mended."

"You will spoil her."

"Have you seen what she can do?" Inge said.

"She can sew."

"Saying that Lida can sew is like saying Wagner can compose a pretty tune. I'll show you." She slipped off the fur coat and showed him her monogram.

I was astounded that Inge would stand up for me in this way.

He looked at it dismissively. "It cannot be difficult to sew a few letters in place."

Inge's eyes flashed with anger. She looked over to me. "Go, Lida. I shall see you tomorrow morning."

I stepped out and closed the door behind me, but I was curious what she was going to say to Officer Schmidt without me there. I cupped my ear against the door and got wisps of the exchange. She must have shown him my other work. I caught words like, "deft tiny hands . . . attention to detail . . . patient." There was a pause in the conversation and I didn't want to be caught eavesdropping, so I left.

When I got to Barracks 7 it was empty, so I folded up the shirt and slipped it under my pillow. I went to the bathhouse and wash house, then back to the barracks. Zenia came in moments later, so exhausted that she collapsed onto her bunk with just a nod in my direction. She pulled her covers up to her chin and groaned in relief.

I pulled the shirt from under my pillow and sat on the edge of her bunk. "I have a surprise for you, Zenia," I said, holding it out.

She looked at the cloth and asked. "What is that?"

"Open it," I said, barely able to contain my excitement. I shook out the shirt so that it opened.

Zenia's eyes widened. "You didn't steal that, I hope."

I shook my head. "Inge gave it to me. A present for my stitch work."

"That is wonderful," said Zenia. "It is so much better than the tattered dress you're wearing."

"But Zenia, this is for you!"

Zenia propped herself up on her elbow and stared into my eyes. "You cannot give this to me. You worked so hard for it."

"Your dress is falling apart," I said. "You need this more than I do."

Zenia blinked back tears. "She should have given you something for yourself — a pair of shoes, or something to eat." She looked down at my scab-encrusted feet. "Maybe you should rip this into strips to wrap your feet with."

"You know they wouldn't last long," I told her. "Besides, I want you to have this. I have a good smock that I wear all day when I'm working, and it's clean in the laundry, so my feet are healing. Do you want to be walking around naked? Your dress is not likely to last much longer."

"Thank you, Lida, thank you." Zenia reached out and gripped my hand. "We can save what's left of my own dress for patching."

She slipped into the shirt and even though she was taller than me, it was still huge on her — we were all not much more than skeletons, after all. She took it off. We were trusted with needle and thread, but not scissors, so I carefully tore off the sleeves so I could adjust it, then picked apart the seams on either side of the shirt so I had one big piece of cloth and two smaller pieces. With the big section of material from the back, I stitched a sleeveless dress for Zenia. I was in the midst of all this sewing when the other girls entered the barracks.

Kataryna picked up the two front panels of the shirt and held them up to me. "There's more than enough to make yourself a new dress out of this. Do you need the buttons?"

I shook my head. While I finished up Zenia's seams, Kataryna picked at the button threads with the sharp end of a sewing needle. Once the buttons were all removed, she stitched the two front sections together. My sleeveless dress needed to be several inches shorter than Zenia's, which meant that there was plenty of cloth left over. We worked at it gingerly so the cloth would tear straight.

With these bits and scraps of sturdy blue flannel, plus my old dress and what was left of Zenia's old outfit, Mary and the others were able to patch their own clothing. Every single girl in Barracks 7 got a bit of cloth. I fell asleep with a smile on my lips for the first time in a very long while. It had been a good day. I dreamt that my mother was bending over me, brushing my forehead with her lips. "Beauty can be found anywhere," she whispered.

I longed to open my eyes and see my real mother, hovering over me, keeping me safe. The dream was so real that I could almost feel her warm breath on my cheek. Mama's face dissolved and was suddenly replaced by

Luka's. "Stay safe, little sister," he said. His lips continued to move but I could no longer hear the words.

"Luka!" I cried. "What are you saying?" My eyes flew open.

The image had been so real that I almost expected Luka to be hovering over me, but he wasn't there. I was thankful that I had gone to see him in the hospital, to know that he was safe. Dreams can so quickly turn to nightmares, after all.

Chapter Eleven

Roll Call

The next day at roll call, several prisoners complimented the girls of Barracks 7 on our nice clothing. It thrilled me to see everyone look so happy.

Officer Schmidt made us all stand at attention for longer than usual. It was drizzling rain and we each stood rigidly. My feet ached from the damp.

The rain didn't bother him, though — a soldier scampered behind him as he walked, holding a huge black umbrella over his head.

My new blue dress was soaked through and every bone in my body ached. I was looking forward to drying out in the laundry.

Officer Schmidt walked up and down our rows, examining each of us carefully, making note of the new patchwork. When he got to Zenia, he stopped.

"Your dress. Where did you get it?"

Zenia lowered her eyes and looked at her muddy feet. "A friend gave it to me."

He grunted. He continued his inspection. When he got to me, he stopped again.

"Nice dress, little seamstress," he said. "That one shirt went far. Why didn't you keep the whole thing for yourself?"

My mouth refused to form words. Officer Schmidt continued to stand in front of me. "Speak up," he said.

"It makes me happy to share," I blurted.

And then the officer did something that shocked me. He smiled. He rested one finger on my shoulder and said, "You were getting a bit too comfortable in the laundry. You have a new assignment."

He reached into the depths of his uniform jacket and pulled out an Ostarbeiter identification paper. He handed it to me, saying, "Today, you go on the train. You will need this."

It was the first time I had seen my own identification paper. I knew from the other girls that we were supposed to have them with us at all times if we left the compound. Getting caught without papers could mean death. Since I had always worked inside the complex itself, Officer Schmidt had never given my OST paper to me before.

I folded the paper quickly and slipped it into my dress pocket to keep it relatively dry. I was devastated that he was moving me. Inge treated me well now and it was so pleasant in the laundry. To go into the city was something I dreaded. It was bombed regularly, after all.

Officer Schmidt read out a list of newly reassigned labourers, including Zenia, and told us that the policemen on the train would have the listings of our new jobs.

A whistle shrilled as the train approached the gates.

"You are dismissed," shouted Officer Schmidt.

I stood in the long lineup to get on the train. There were two policemen under a lamppost at the gate. One ticked off people's names on his clipboard as they passed him. The other stood with a rifle casually leaning against his shoulder.

When it was my turn, the policeman's brow crinkled. "You've not travelled to work before. What is your name?"

"Lida Ferezuk." I took out my identification paper and showed it to him.

He scanned the list of names on his clipboard. "Ah," he said. He pointed to a train car that was four units down. "That's the one for you."

I walked along a well-used path beside the tracks until I got to the correct train car. I was expecting it to be a cattle car like the one we arrived in, but this car had two rows of wooden benches and an aisle down the middle. Most of the seats had already been taken, and as I looked around for a place to sit, I was surprised to see regular people in the car: a grey-haired civilian with his coat unbuttoned, revealing paint-splattered overalls; a plain looking woman with her hair twisted in a bun, wearing a feathered green hat that looked like it was meant for someone else. Beside her sat a young girl whose blond curls spilled out over her blue sweater. That girl reminded me so much of Larissa that I had to look away before I began to weep.

"Lida! Here!" Zenia's voice. I scanned the car. There she was, sitting near the back by herself. Across the aisle from her sat Kataryna and Natalia from our barracks. Mary, the school girl I had thought was a teacher, sat in front of her with an older labourer whose name I didn't know.

I made my way down the aisle and sat beside Zenia, setting my bowl, cup and spoon on my lap.

After having an assignment away from the others for so long, it was a nice change to be with some people I knew, and of all the girls in my barracks, I liked Zenia the best.

"We'll be together," I said. "Won't that be wonderful?"

Zenia regarded me, one brow arched. "There is no such thing as wonderful here."

"You're right, Zenia. But I am still looking forward to working with you."

"Yes, that is a good thing. Let's just hope our new jobs aren't too difficult."

The last to get into the compartment were two policemen. One of them slid the door shut and a policeman outside bolted it. The train shuddered and screeched and soon we were speeding away. I watched out the window, hungry for a view of something that wasn't surrounded by barbed wire.

The train stopped at stations along the way and I watched through the window as policemen with clipboards would approach the train. The labourers would be herded out, and a policeman from the train would give a sheet of paper to the new policeman, who clipped it to his board and checked off the workers one by one. Some of them were loaded into the backs of trucks and others walked in single file, led by a German in civilian clothing.

Zenia had been travelling this route for some time. "Who are those people taking the labourers away?" I asked her.

"Factory owners, quarry managers, business owners," she replied.

"I thought we were forced workers for the Nazis."

"These businessmen pay the government for the privilege of using us," replied Zenia bitterly. "I am sure they find it quite a convenience to have slaves."

Her comment made me wonder what these regular Germans thought about us. Did they think we had done something wrong and were being punished? Or did they even know that their government captured people from other countries and made them work for Germany?

As our train idled at a later stop, we watched as a cluster of near-dead men who wore yellow stars on their striped rags were forced into the back of a truck by a soldier with a billy club. We were treated terribly, but one glance told us these Jewish people had it even worse. Were they fed at all? A shiver ran down my back, as if someone had stepped on my grave.

Our stop was the last. The whole time I had been on the train I hadn't heard the sound of bomber planes overhead. It wasn't because they had stopped, but because the train's chugging was so loud. As soon as I stepped outside, the familiar high-pitched whine of American bombs was all I could hear. The ground trembled when one hit and I would see a puff of smoke in the near distance. It didn't matter how often I heard bombs, I could never get used to them.

I stepped in line behind Mary and waited to be processed. The sun was shining over the top of a mountain range in the distance. These sharp grey rocks were nothing like our mountains back home. Ours had gentle rolling slopes covered with trees and grass. These jutted up into the heavens like weapons.

As I waited in line, I felt the folded ridges of my identification paper in my pocket. I could not lose this. I pulled it out and for the first time took a good look at the photograph. Was that really me? It was less than a year ago, but I looked so young and innocent. Aside from the whip slash on my face, the shaved head and the bug bites, I had looked almost healthy. I put my hand up to my cheekbone where the cut had been. The wound had closed over, but the skin was so thin that I could feel each of my teeth. I put my hand up to my hair. It was longer now, but standing up in tufts. Washing it with the harsh bleaching powder and cold water was essential to keep the lice away, but it burned my scalp and matted my hair.

The paper was snatched out of my hand. I looked up. The policeman.

"You are Lida Ferezuk?"

I nodded.

He found my name on his list and put a check mark beside it. "You go over there to Frau Zanger," he said, pointing with his pencil to a woman in a tailored blue suit.

I tried not to stare at her, but it was hard not to. First of all, the only other women at the train station were either frumpy looking mothers with children, or they were slave labourers. I could tell by the cut of this woman's suit that it was custom-made to show off her narrow waist. The material was expensive — I suspected it was a fine woven wool from England. Mama once had a customer who got her clothing from England, and she would bring it in to us for alterations. Frau Zanger's outfit reminded me of that woman's.

The policeman showed her his clipboard and together she ran through our names: me, Kataryna, Zenia, Mary, Natalia and a woman I didn't recognize, named Bibi. "Very good," she said in German, but with an unfamiliar accent. "And you're sure these all have steady hands?"

The policeman flipped through the pages in his clipboard. He pointed to one name. They both looked up at Zenia, who had removed the bandages on her arm, but the scratches were still vivid. "I don't know why they gave you one who is injured."

"If she's not any good, I'll just get rid of her."

"Yes, ma'am. I do know that these six were all hand-selected for you. Should I load them up?"

"Yes, Hans. I'll meet you at the factory."

She walked up to a long black car that was idling beside the station building. A uniformed man jumped out of the driver's seat and ran to the back door on the opposite side, opening it wide just as she got to it. He closed her door once she stepped in, then he got back in and sped away.

The workman loaded the six of us onto the open back of a pickup truck. The truck bed was wet with rain and there were no benches, so we had no choice but to sit down in the puddles. We huddled together with Zenia in the middle to keep her from falling on her scratches as we were driven away from the station. What had we been hand-selected for?

As we were driven through the busy city streets, I could not see a single building that had been untouched by bombs. I watched in awe as we passed a husband and wife sipping tea at a kitchen table in a second-floor flat — only the flat had no walls and no ceiling. Below them the building was in rubble as well. I guess they were thankful they at least had a kitchen.

From the camp, I had listened to the American and British bombs going off non-stop since I had arrived there. But listening to bombs in the distance was quite different from witnessing the damage close up. I knew we were in more danger here in the city, but I was exhilarated to see that the Nazis weren't doing so well. How I longed for the war to be over. Then I could find my sister and we could both go home.

The driver manoeuvred around fallen stonework from a bombed church, which sent us careening to one side in the back of the truck. I tried to keep Zenia upright, but when I lost my balance, she landed painfully on her injured arm. I watched clean, well-fed men and women wearing decent clothing walking along on the sidewalks, stepping through bombed fragments of lumber, stone and brick. Looking at them made me feel dirty and insignificant. None of them seemed to notice us at all. I guess they had got used to seeing truckloads of scrawny labourers passing by.

The truck pulled up to the entrance of a large U-shaped building made of yellow brick. It seemed to have miraculously escaped most of the air raids, although an outbuilding was nothing more than fresh rubble of twisted metal and brick. The large arched windows of the main building had all shattered and were boarded up with wood. Shards of glass still hung from parts of the framework like jagged teeth. I suspected that damage was just from the ground shaking rather than a direct bomb hit.

"Oh no," said Zenia. "I was hoping to be assigned somewhere else."

"This is the metalworks factory that was just bombed?" I asked.

"I was working in there." She pointed to the flattened outbuilding.

What part of this factory would we be working in? How long would it stay standing? I had heard that factory buildings were a magnet for bombs.

"It's safer than you think," Zenia said, reading the look of fear in my eyes. "The main building has been marked on the roof with the symbol for Hospital and it has largely escaped the bombing. I bet my building got hit by mistake."

The workman opened up the back of the truck. We got out and he ushered the six of us through the front entrance. I was grateful to be in a dry place, but I wished I was back at the laundry. We stood in a reception area. To one side was a glassed-in office, with a large double-sided desk. Two healthy looking blond women faced one another, one pecking at a typewriter with two fingers, while the other tackled forms, one by one, filling them out with a pen.

Frau Zanger had one hand clasped around the knob of a battered wooden door that stood beside a larger door. She was having a heated conversation with a woman in a wraparound white smock. The woman's head was bowed respectfully, but her hands were clenched at her side. Frau Zanger stabbed one finger in our direction and said to her, "I don't care how much other work you need to do. You will train these workers now."

Then she turned to us. "In there, all of you," she snapped.

She opened the door and ushered the supervisor and us up the stairs and into a wire-mesh second-floor catwalk. She didn't follow us. Down below we could see the metalworks factory as the day shift came in and the night shift shuffled out. Although we were a storey above the machines, we were still enveloped in the mechanical thrumming, banging, clanging and grinding. Even the wooden floor of the walkway vibrated. I looked down at one contraption that had a huge sledgehammer device on a swinging arm. I watched the labourer at that station place a piece of metal down on a flat tray. The mechanized sledgehammer slammed down, turning the metal piece into the shape of a small bowl. As the sledgehammer rose again, the worker swept the stamped bowl onto a conveyor belt and placed the next piece of metal in the same spot on the tray.

It seemed to me that it would be easy to have a finger or a hand on the tray at the wrong time, yet the worker was using her bare hands. The force of that sledgehammer could send bits of metal into her face, even her eyes. I guess it didn't matter to the owners.

The metal bowls travelled down the conveyor belt and were picked up by women operating machines with spinning stone wheels. As they smoothed and ground the sides of the metal bowls, they were enveloped in a cloud of dust.

Zenia was in front of me as we walked single file behind the supervisor. "Was that your job before?" I asked, pointing at the grinding machines.

"That's what I was doing, but in the outbuilding we were working with different-shaped metal," she said.

Other machines produced cylindrical pieces of metal, some as long as my arm. The labourers looked almost like machines themselves, except for their gaunt appearance and their exhaustion.

When we had walked the length of the factory, we followed the German supervisor through another door and into a low-ceilinged white room. It had a wooden table and attached benches at one end and an open tiled area with a long metal trough for washing at the other. A small pail of bleaching powder was hooked onto one of the taps. There was a single flush toilet off to one side.

"Put your eating utensils on the table," she said. "You will wash your arms and hands carefully and then I will inspect you."

We did as we were told. I used the dreaded bleaching powder sparingly, but the water was gloriously hot. Zenia washed her scrapes gingerly with the stinging powder. Her left hand was slightly swollen, but she seemed to have good control over her fingers. I hoped that the supervisor would deem her useful.

When we were finished, we lined up in a row, our hands dripping water as we stood at the edge of the tiled area.

"Hold them out," she ordered. She inspected the palms of our hands first, then turned each one, examining our fingernails closely. "You pass . . . you pass . . . you pass . . . "

My hands were clean enough, so I stood to one side. Bibi was wearing a wedding ring. "This must come off," said the woman.

The ring was loose on Bibi's finger and I was surprised that she had managed to keep it for so long. "Madame Manager," she said, blinking back tears, "I have never removed this ring. It is all that I have left of my husband."

"I don't want your ring," said the woman. "For your own protection, there can be no metal in the room you'll be working in. Leave the ring on the table with your eating utensils."

"Might someone steal it, just sitting there?" asked Bibi.

"The other workers do not come into this area," said the woman.

When she got to Zenia, she made a clicking noise with her tongue. "How do you expect to work with swollen fingers?"

Zenia opened and closed the fingers on her left hand. "My hand works just fine," she said.

The woman shook her head in disgust. "Why did they even send you to me? Couldn't they find anyone better than a half cripple?"

"I am one of the bomb survivors," said Zenia. "If you ask Foreman Lichstaedler, he will tell you what a good worker I am."

"Lichstaedler did not survive the attack," said the supervisor. "I'll give you a try." Her eyes landed on Zenia's neck. "That cross — it's metal. Take it off."

Zenia drew the leather strap over her neck and placed my precious cross on the table.

The woman led us through the next door into yet another white room, this one empty, save for a table stacked with clean grey smocks.

"You will notice that these smocks have no metal snaps

or clips and no dangling belts. They're washed daily and they wrap around you and tie at the back. It is important that they are worn snugly, but your labourer badges must still be visible. Do any of you have metal on your clothing?" She examined each girl's dress, looking for snaps, zippers or metal clips, but none of us had any.

She gave us each a square of grey cloth. "You wear this over your hair." She took out an extra one and said to Zenia, "Hold out your arm," then expertly covered Zenia's injury.

Where was it that we were working? We were in a factory, yet we were being prepared as if for a hospital.

The supervisor checked her pocket and pulled out a pen with a metal tip and set it on the table. "One last chance," she said. "If you have any metal, take it off now." She looked at us with one eyebrow arched. None of us had anything else to give her.

She ushered us into the next room.

Chapter Twelve

Making Bombs

One entire wall was draped off. On a wooden table were the metal bowls like those I had seen being made in the factory. There were long metal tubes, wires and other pieces as well, all organized neatly on that same table. Hadn't she told us that there was supposed to be no metal in the room? All of those pieces were made of metal. A wooden barrel rested on the floor beside a second table, its wooden cover was stamped *Schießpulver*.

Gunpowder?

A low shelf that was nearly the length of the room was positioned in front of the curtained wall. Lined up neatly on its surface were bundles of what looked like a kind of metal straw.

What were we making in this room?

A second table held a weigh scale and an array of porcelain measuring spoons. A separate table was mounted with a mechanical device that looked like a smaller version of the automatic sledgehammer in the factory. A wide wooden rack that reached almost as high as the ceiling took up most of the wall beside the entrance.

"In this room, you will be making bombs," said the supervisor. "The reason for no metal is because you could create a spark and that could cause an explosion."

Making *bombs?* I suddenly felt weak at the knees. I had been so afraid of Allied bombs hitting us, yet our fate here was even worse. They expected us to make bombs for the Nazis, our enemies? Here I thought I had been so smart, staying alive by pretending I was older, and demonstrating my value in the hopes of getting a good job. Marika was the luckiest. At least she had died innocent.

My eyes locked onto the metal components arranged on the table. They had looked so harmless in the factory down below. But now as I looked at them, I could see how they all fitted together like the pattern pieces of a dress.

The woman walked over to the table of metal parts and, with both hands, positioned one of the cylindrical pieces so it stood upright. "This is the body of the bomb." She turned it so we could see the hollow inside. "You will seal the bottom with this — " she held up a different metal part " — then fill the hollow part with *Kordit.*" She set the cylindrical piece back down on the table and walked over to the array of straw-like bundles. "You must be very careful when you insert this metal straw. It is an explosive."

The woman's mouth formed the words and I tried to pay attention to her demonstration, but I was so horrified that the room swirled. How could she ask us to do this? Didn't she know that we all were hoping and praying that the Allies would win? If Hitler won, even if we somehow managed to survive, the rest of our lives would be as slaves. If the Allies conquered Hitler, then they could fight Stalin for us and we might live. How could they force us to make these weapons?

I took gulping breaths to keep from fainting as she explained what we had to do. I looked over at Zenia. Her face was ashen. Natalia's eyes were wide and her jaw was slack. We were all thinking the same thing.

"Each of you was chosen for your deft fingers," said the supervisor. "And in case you're thinking of sabotaging these bombs, don't bother. You're being watched."

She walked over to the drape and pulled it open. A man in a white smock sat at a wooden table. He waved to her, then looked back down at the papers he had been working on. Behind him was a giant wall clock, showing that it was 6:45 a.m.

"That is thick laminated glass," she said, tapping the partition with her fingernail. "And the rest of the factory is separated from you by several rooms. If you have an explosion, the only people to die will be yourselves and this is the only room that will be damaged."

The woman stayed all morning, supervising us as we learned how to assemble the bombs. My job was to precisely measure out the exact amount of powdered explosive needed for the nose of each bomb — those bowl-like pieces of metal. Too much could cause an immediate explosion and too little would make the bomb unstable. Bibi delicately inserted the long wire-like fuse, making sure that not a single grain of explosive came in contact with it. Zenia inserted the long straw-like *Kordit* into the body of the bomb and Kataryna tightened all the components together with a special metal-free hand tool. It was a delicate procedure. There were bits of explosive dust in the air. One spark and we would all be finished.

The worst job fell to Mary. She was selected to operate the hammering machine. Unlike the automatic one we had seen in the factory, this machine had a hand lever. Once all of the components were assembled into a bomb, all of us would help her mount each one onto the front plate of her machine. These bombs weighed more than I did and they were smooth and cold and hard to grip. It was terrifying for us to carry them. I would look into each of my friends' eyes and try not to breathe as we gingerly moved each bomb from the assembly table to Mary's machine. Once the bomb was in place, Mary would lower the hammer slowly, gently increasing the pressure until the various edges and ridges snapped into place. To keep the bomb cool while she did this, the outside of it was washed with a milky substance that stayed liquid even though it was colder than ice.

Natalia's task was to keep that liquid flowing. It wasn't as precise a job as some of the others, but it was very uncomfortable, as she had to hold the icy container with her bare hands. We were indoors, yet her fingers looked frostbitten.

The supervisor watched us like an eagle all morning, making sure that all of us could handle our jobs with accuracy and speed. When the clock in the room showed noon, she said, "Finish what you are doing, then follow me."

She led us back out to the white room and we removed our smocks. "You don't eat your meal with the other factory workers," she said as we followed her out the next door. "You will eat in this room at the table, but first you must wash off the explosive powder."

For the second time that day, we scrubbed with the dreaded bleaching powder. As she was inspecting our hands, a man came in, carrying two sloshing pails, one large and one small. The woman left the room for her own lunch. We lined up and he ladled us each a bowl of our usual turnip and water soup from the larger pail, then filled our drinking tins with something hot that he called coffee. When it was Natalia's turn, he served her from the smaller pail. I looked longingly at the potatoes floating in her Polish soup but I tried to put it out of my mind. Letting her eat more in front of us was a torture for her as well.

"Will you look at that," said the man, tilting the larger bucket for us to see. "There's still some Russian soup left."

My heart soared. "Sir," I said, "perhaps you could give us each a small bit more soup and then you wouldn't have such a heavy load to carry back down to the *Kantine.*"

"I could never do that," he said. "If I were caught giving extra food to Ostarbeiters, I would be punished."

He picked up the pail and carried it over to our washing area. He poured that precious soup into the toilet and flushed. "There," he said. "Now I don't have to carry any of it back."

I felt like pummelling him with my fists. How cruel could a person be, to throw out food in front of starving people? And who would have known if he had given us the soup instead? We certainly would not have told anyone. I didn't want him to see how much his action affected me, so I kept my face emotionless until he stepped out the door. As soon as he was gone, I lay my head down on my arms and wept.

The supervisor didn't come back in the afternoon, but the man behind the partition stood at the glass and watched our every movement, writing things down in a notebook from time to time.

It scared me to think of how many bombs we were assembling. As each one was finished, we would stop what we were doing and carry it like a baby to the wooden rack by the door. By the end of the day, the rack was full. How many people would be killed because of our work? It made me shudder to think of it.

The man from behind the glass met us in the outer room when the whistle blew, to watch us wash away any stray flecks of gunpowder. I was thankful — and also a bit surprised — to see that Bibi's wedding ring was where she had left it, and so was my crucifix.

We were subdued on the train ride back to the work camp. I could hear the incessant *whizz-boom* of the Americans bombing, and it was so close to us that the rail car shook. Who made the bombs in Britain and America? Surely they had no slaves? But whoever was doing it must have been feeling as bad as we were.

One good thing about making bombs is that we six were able to wash in an uncrowded bathroom before getting on the train. That meant that we didn't have to wait in line to use the wash house at the camp. When I got off the train, Juli was there, an anxious look in her eyes. She fell in step beside me and walked me back to Barracks 7. I didn't have to be a mind reader to realize that she had something to tell me.

Juli followed me in and sat beside me on my bunk. She had never done that before. I could see her eyes taking in the room with curiosity. "This is just like my own barracks," she said, then her eyes locked onto mine. "What job do they have you doing?"

"Making bombs."

Her eyebrows rose in surprise. "Where is that?"

"In the same complex as that bombed metalworks factory. Our room is in a separate area."

"Oh, Lida. How awful."

"It's my punishment for being good with my hands."

Juli looked at her lap. Tears splattered down her cheeks. "It could be worse . . . "

"It's not that," said Juli, looking at me with tear-filled eyes. "It's Luka," she sobbed. "He is gone."

Is that what my dream had meant? This I could not take. Anything but Luka dying. I took her by the shoulders. "But I saw him with my own eyes yesterday. He was healthy."

She looked at me then, her eyes shining with tears. "You don't understand," she said. "He didn't die. He has somehow disappeared."

"*Escaped?*"

Juli nodded. "The medical staff is in a frenzy. They've marked him as dead to save face, but I know he didn't die."

I didn't want to ask her exactly how she knew that. And it didn't really matter. He had escaped! My heart soared. The fact of his escape was the best news I had heard in a long time.

"Do you think he will make it?" I asked.

"Hard to say. A farmer might take him in."

I wrapped my arms around Juli and hugged her tight. "Thank you, Juli! You have given me hope."

Zenia, Natalia and Kataryna came into the barracks while Juli was there. When I told them the good news, Zenia said, "I wonder if *we* could escape."

"And go where?" asked Juli.

None of us had an answer.

After she left we were all wrapped in our own thoughts. How long could I bear to make bombs? The idea that escape might be possible gave me something positive to think about.

Chapter Thirteen

Like Rats

All night I listened to Allied bombers blast the country-side. As sirens shrilled, I prayed that Luka would be safe. When I finally got to sleep I dreamed that bombs were everywhere. They lined up for soup in the *Kantine* with me and they lay down in the bunk beside me. There were so many bombs in the air that the sky looked grey. I dreamed of Larissa, her arms holding a bomb like it was a baby. I woke up weeping.

When we got to our work area the next day, our wooden rack of bombs had been emptied. I figured that removing them must be a job for someone on the night shift. I watched my own hands measure out explosives and carefully fill the nose of each bomb, making sure there wasn't a grain too much gunpowder or too little, acutely aware of that man behind the glass. It was almost as if those hands didn't belong to me.

The third day was the same as the first and the second, but the monotony of building bombs did not relieve the terror. Each night I tossed and turned, wondering about who would be dead because of me.

✤ ✤ ✤

I didn't think it would ever happen, but after a few weeks we all somehow did get used to making bombs. And we breathed easier as time passed and our building was not hit. The aerial camouflage seemed to be working.

We six did not talk about our work at lunchtime or on the train ride back. We looked forward to our moments of privacy, like those few minutes in our barracks while the others were washing up. Sometimes on a Saturday afternoon or on Sunday we were able to gather together as well, but during those times Natalia was gone, working for hire. But since she would come back with tidbits of information as well as food for us, it became a Sunday night ritual for the six of us to gather together inside the wash house just before curfew.

On the last Sunday in October, Natalia looked especially pleased with herself as she stepped into the wash house. She sat down on the edge of the trough and we gathered around her in anticipation.

"You will never believe what I managed to get this time," she said, her eyes shining. She reached into an inconspicuous pocket in the depths of her threadbare dress, pulled out a small flat package and folded back the paper. Brown sugar!

Curling the paper into a cone, she said, "Hold out your hand."

She shook out a small pyramid of brown sugar on my palm. I licked it up, revelling in the burst of sweetness. When was the last time I had eaten anything so good? Not in the years of Soviet rule, and certainly not since the Nazis had come.

All at once I remembered my last bit of sweetness. That Nazi woman dressed in brown who gave Larissa and me candies in exchange for information . . .

I swallowed down the sugar that coated my tongue, but the memory hung there. Had I not taken those candies, maybe Larissa and I would still be safe. And my own grandmother — was she dead because of me? My eyes filled with tears. I blinked hard, trying to erase the disturbing images. I looked over to Zenia. She held her hand in front of her face, palm up.

"This reminds me of the gunpowder we use in the bombs," she said.

Kataryna had licked every last speck of sugar from her own palm. She stared at Zenia's grains.

"This . . . this brown sugar is the wrong texture . . . and it's not dark enough," she said. "I think the dirt outside this wash house looks more like the gunpowder . . . "

Gunpowder. Grains that looked like the explosive but weren't . . .

"What would — " Natalia began, then stopped.

We all looked at her.

"What would happen if we put some dirt into the bombs?" said Natalia.

My heart nearly stopped beating. What a bold thought. "They wouldn't work so well, is my guess," said Zenia. She still hadn't eaten the sugar on her palm.

"How would we sneak it in?" asked Kataryna.

"The same way I brought in the sugar," said Natalia. "In our pockets."

We looked at each other solemnly. Could it work? Would we be caught? It was hard to know.

Was it worth the chance? Definitely.

Kataryna looked at Natalia, her eyes alight with a new idea. "If I ease up on the hammer machine early," she said, "I think the bombs would fail to snap together all the way. They might fall apart instead of exploding."

"We have many ways of ruining the bombs," I said. "But we are watched. Always watched."

✧ ✧ ✧

As fall turned towards winter, we noticed subtle changes all around. Bombs had been falling all day and night for months, but now the sky was black with Allied bomber planes. We heard that entire German cities had been destroyed. At the work camp, some of the policemen hung up their uniforms and left. The ones who stayed became even more cruel than they had been. It was like their war losses were our fault. Once, when Officer Schmidt was annoyed by a prisoner's answer at roll call, he cocked his gun and shot the man on the spot. We were all afraid to breathe.

On our way to and from the city, I would look out the window and try to make sense of what I saw. Waves of ragged refugees walked through city streets. Some were starving like us, but others looked like they had recently been well fed. The few Germans who still rode on the train with us would whisper among themselves and I would try to listen, to find out what was going on. From what I could hear, the Soviets were pushing the Nazis back. As the battleground moved closer to us, whole villages and towns were being destroyed. People who survived fled west — away from the fighting — but farther into Nazi territory.

One icy evening in November when I stepped off the train after work, Juli met me, her eyes rimmed with red.

"I have something for you," she said. "Come quickly."

She grabbed me by the hand and pulled me along to her barracks. We stepped inside. It was empty save for us. She knelt in front of her bed, which was a bottom bunk close to the heater at the back, reached in and drew out a pair of worn leather shoes that were made for a woman.

"Put these on and let's get out of here before anyone else comes in."

Shoes were like gold in the camp. Where had Juli got these? I didn't stop to think about it, but slipped my feet inside. They were roomy, but I didn't mind. My feet were swollen and the shoes felt warm and solid. I followed Juli out the door, stepping gingerly, trying to re-teach myself how to walk in shoes.

I noticed a truck idling by the entrance to the hospital.

"What is that truck for?"

Juli's eyes filled with tears. "Don't go there."

But of course I did.

The back of the truck was stacked with the gaunt bodies of dead slaves, many with faces frozen in painful contortions. I recognized one as the woman who had replaced me helping Inge in the laundry. She was barefoot. I looked down at my feet and knew where my shoes had come from. My heart felt like it could burst with guilt. Here I was, benefiting from someone else's death.

"Better you have the shoes than they get buried," Juli murmured.

I said a silent prayer for the woman whose shoes I wore, then looked at the others in the truck. They were mostly strangers. Where had these people come from and why were they now all dead?

"What happened?" I asked Juli.

"The Nazis are retreating in the east, and camps there are being overrun by the Soviets." She nodded back towards the truck. "The Nazis shipped those prisoners away from a work camp just before it was liberated by the Soviets. The prisoners arrived on a train this morning, starving and nearly frozen. Officer Schmidt decided that they wouldn't be useful workers and he didn't want to waste food on them. He ordered the cook to put poison into today's Russian soup." She blinked back tears. "All of the eastern workers who were in the camp today have died."

Even though my stomach was empty, bile rose in my throat. Should I be thankful that my friends and I had our soup at the factory instead of at the camp? Should I be thankful for my shoes? It was mere chance that I wasn't one of those corpses on the back of the truck.

"I had heard about these mass poisonings before, but it seemed so impossible, even for the Nazis, I thought it was a rumour," said Juli, brushing away a tear with the back of her hand. "I've been told that is why the Russian soup always has a separate ladle."

I looked down at my new shoes and then back towards the truck. "The Nazis will pay for this," I vowed to Juli. "They should think twice before asking slaves to make bombs."

Chapter Fourteen

Scrap of Light

When 1944 arrived we did nothing in the camp to mark the new year. Maybe the camp guards and the police had extra food. Maybe they toasted each others' good health. For us it was a usual Friday night. I went to bed and tried to sleep. I tried not to think of the possibility of spending another year making bombs for Hitler.

Ukrainian Christmas Eve was the following Thursday, and those of us in Barracks 7 sang hymns together as we lay in our bunks, shivering under our covers. Just a year ago I had been with Larissa and my grandmother. Back then I thought things couldn't get worse. I was an orphan, after all. Looking back now, I realized how I should have been thankful for all that we had — not much food, no parents, but a roof over our heads and the love of our grandmother.

As January blizzards blew outside, I was grateful for my shoes. The man behind the glass stopped paying so much attention to us. He would bring in the daily newspaper and read every page. I would glance over and see him engrossed in the latest news from the Front, not looking our way for fifteen minutes at a time. Every once in a while he would leave. Sometimes he would be gone for only a minute or so, but there were times when he was gone for half a day.

We sensed the war was turning very bad for the Nazis. Some of the changes were subtle: German supervisors in the factory simply stopped showing up. In their place would be German housewives who seemed wholly unprepared for the job they were supposed to do, or boys in Hitler Youth uniforms, who were eager but untrained. I lived in hope that the man behind the glass would abandon his post as well, but although his absences became longer, and he paid scant attention to us while he was there, he always seemed to eventually come back.

But we had the opportunity for sabotage in those times that he was gone. Each morning now we filled our pockets with dirt from the camp. Even with the supervisor reading the paper, it was possible to slip my hand into my pocket and fill the metal bowl with dirt instead of gunpowder.

Natalia's trick could only be done when the supervisor was gone. She would dampen the inside cavities of the bombs with the icy fluid. The gunpowder that was inserted after that was spoiled — we hoped.

One morning we came in and the supervisor was gone. On his desk was a day-old newspaper and a dirty coffee cup. Perhaps he would finally not come in at all. We used his early absence to sabotage bombshell after bombshell. Natalia gave the barrel of gunpowder a good soaking with her cooling fluid. She sprayed fluid all over the straw-like

Kordit as well. We made the bombs out of this destroyed material, and included scraps of paper upon which Bibi wrote in several languages, *Dear Allies, this is all that we can do for you now.*

Shortly before lunch the supervisor came back. We had just closed up one of the tampered bombs. I had a hard time keeping my face serious, I felt so exultant. I was positively giddy with the fact that we had succeeded in destroying so many bombs. Had he bothered to glance into our room, he might have noticed the *Kordit* glistening, but he didn't look. Instead he opened up his briefcase with trembling fingers and began frantically stuffing papers into it from his desk. Without glancing at us even once, he left, stray papers fluttering behind him.

With him gone, we continued to make fake bombs. At midday we joked together as we hung up our smocks, then washed up as usual. I was grateful when the kitchen worker came in with our soup. So many Germans seemed to be fleeing. Our turnip soup was not filling, but it was the only thing keeping us alive.

Just as I held a spoonful of watery turnip to my lips, the room was enveloped in a loud boom. A gust of air whooshed in from above with such force that it blew me off my chair. My spoon flew out of my hand and smacked against the wall. I scrambled to my feet, trying to make sense of what had just happened. When I looked up at the ceiling, my heart stood still. Where grey ceiling tiles should have been, there was a huge star-shaped hole. And that's when I looked immediately below the hole — our table. Sticking up in the middle of it was the narrow end of a small bomb, fins pointing upward.

Time stood still. For one long moment I stared at that bomb, comparing it to the ones we were making. This was similar in size and colour, but teardrop-shaped instead of oblong. All at once I came to my senses. This was a bomb that had been dropped on us. It hadn't exploded . . . yet.

"Out!" I screamed. "Now!"

The other girls seemed as stunned and confused as I was.

I scrambled to my feet and ran to the door that connected our room to the catwalk above the factory. I pulled on the handle. Mercifully, it was unlocked. Zenia, Mary, Bibi, Natalia, Kataryna and I all flew out, yanking the door closed behind us. We stumbled down the catwalk as quickly as our feet would take us. When we were nearly at the other end of the factory, the ground shook so violently that I was knocked off my feet, my friends tumbling around me.

I turned to look. The force of the explosion had blasted our lunchroom door off its hinges. Hot air and flames licked down the catwalk towards us.

"Get up! Up up!" screamed Kataryna, pulling on my arms. I stumbled to my feet, as did Zenia behind me. Mary was the farthest down the catwalk and she got to the exit door first. She pulled it open and we all tumbled out into the main entryway of the factory and collapsed in a heap, smoke billowing out behind us.

Hands pulled at us. Air-raid sirens blared, but I could hear the rumble of bricks and mortar falling around us. All at once I gulped in cold fresh air. I looked up and counted. All six of us were there. We had miraculously survived the bombing.

Young boys with Hitler Youth arm bands herded us away from the building and told us to stand with factory workers from the main wing. We milled about, shocked and frightened, blood trickling from our wounds.

I took huge gulping breaths to calm myself and willed myself not to cry. Zenia and Bibi were standing a few feet apart from the other workers, pointing to part of the factory. I turned to look, and gasped. One third of it had been bombed flat. And where our bomb room had been was now a hollowed-out shell. My first thought was one of frustration — all those sabotaged bombs had been destroyed. All that trickery for nothing. My second thought was exultation. Maybe the bombs didn't get used, but I was sure we had saved many labourers' lives here today because of watering the gunpowder. But then I wondered: how long would it take the officers in charge to realize that had those bombs been real, they'd have exploded when the Allies' bomb hit, and the damage would have been far worse than this? What would they do to us when they realized what we had done to the German bombs?

I looked over at Zenia. She met my eyes and nodded slightly. She was wondering the same thing.

"You. Out of the way."

I looked up. A Nazi officer with an impatient frown on his face was pushing his way through. His black dress uniform was crisply pressed and his boots and brass were so polished that they sparkled in the sunlight despite the smoke. He seemed out of place in the burning rubble.

"You, and you — " he pointed to a couple of the older Hitler Youth. "Get the first-aid kit. You," he said, turning to a factory supervisor, "where is the fire hose?"

Kataryna limped over to where I stood and leaned heavily against my side. "I've sprained my ankle."

In the haze of the smoke, I saw slashes of red. Natalia's scalp had been cut, and Mary's hand.

A long black car sat idling at the entrance of the factory. The officer's, I assumed. I watched as the glass in the rear window rolled down. A woman, her blond curls styled to perfection, stuck her head out. "Franz," she called out. "We will be late for the rally."

The officer glanced her way, then waved his gloved hand as if warding off a fly.

The woman's head disappeared in the depths of the car.

A young girl with blond braids looked out the window. She said something to someone inside. A second blond head appeared.

The sight of her stopped my heart. But where had I seen her before? Right at that moment, she squinted. Her eyes locked onto mine. A look of panic transformed her face and she stretched out her arms to me. She said something that was lost in the tumult, but her lips seemed to say, "Lida, please don't leave me . . ."

Was I dreaming?

I waved, too stunned to even take a step towards her.

She waved back.

Suddenly both blond heads disappeared. I could see the woman scolding them as the window rolled up.

Could that have been Larissa? My Larissa? But in the car of a Nazi officer? No. How could it possibly have been my sister?

Chapter Fifteen

Alone

With the factory bombed out, and complete chaos all around, there was nothing for us to do. Did that mean that we were useless? I hoped not. We were loaded onto the train in haphazard fashion — wounded and uninjured all together — and taken back to the work camp. Zenia sat beside me. Bibi and Natalia huddled together across the aisle, whispering in low voices. There were so few people on the train that Kataryna was stretched across one of the benches fast asleep. Mary sat by herself, staring out the window as the wrecked city and bombed-out countryside chugged by. I think we were all still in shock from our close call with death.

My mind was spinning with the image of that blond girl. Could it have been Larissa? Was my mind playing tricks on me? If it was Larissa, at least she was alive. But alive and living *as a Nazi*?

It would be better for her to be dead.

I was confused and exhausted, hungry and sad. I

closed my eyes and rested my head on Zenia's shoulder.

A deafening double-bang jolted me awake. The train shuddered to a screeching halt. My eyes flew open. Kataryna fell off her bench with a thud. For long moments nothing else happened, but then the compartment filled with billowing smoke. Another bomb? Had we been hit? I ran to the door and pulled on the handle, but it was bolted from the outside. I pounded on it, shouting, "Let us out! Let us out!"

A young boy in civilian clothes but with a Hitler Youth arm band ran up to our door. He stretched up his hand but he was too short to reach the bolt. Smoke enveloped us. I watched out the window as he pulled himself up the ridges on the door as if he were climbing a tree. He unlatched the bolt, then jumped back down onto the ground, running to the next car to open that door the same way. I pushed our door open and fresh air rushed in. Zenia helped Kataryna up off the floor and we all tumbled out, stumbling and tripping in our haste to get away from that train as quickly as we could. I looked up and down the tracks, and saw many gaunt and weary slaves, frightened and tired, some still bleeding, being ordered about by boys who didn't seem much older than I was. It was complete chaos. The six of us stood in a cluster, not knowing what to do.

"I'm not sticking around," said Mary. In one swift movement, she tore off her OST badge and threw it onto the ground. She tugged Bibi by the arm. "Come on," she urged.

Bibi ripped off her badge too, and the two made a run for it.

Where would they go? There was no place safe from the bombing, and escaped slaves could be shot on sight, but I envied their bravery.

I turned to Zenia. "Should we go too?"

She had a terrified look in her eyes. "I don't know what we should do."

In our relatively new blue flannel dresses, we looked less like slave labourers than many of the others, but our scraggly hair and gaunt appearance was a clear giveaway. We were close enough to the camp that we could see the guardhouses. Natalia looked from Zenia to me. "I'm not standing around here," she said. "That train could explode any time now." She looped her hand through the crook of Kataryna's elbow and they slowly began to walk in the direction of the camp, Kataryna limping with her sprained ankle. I followed them. Zenia followed me.

Walking with slippery shoes in the winter is difficult, so I kept my eyes to the ground and tried to avoid the slicks of ice. The four of us were just one link of a chain of people slowly making their way back to the work camp, the smoking train to our side. When we passed the engine car, I paused for a brief moment to stare. The way the bomb had smashed into it made it look like a toy train that a willful child had stomped into bits. Flames licked along the sides and black oily smoke filled the air in a tall spiral above it. I covered my mouth and hurried on. Natalia was right — the whole thing could explode at any moment. With each shivering step I took, I thought of that pampered girl who looked like my sister.

When we finally reached the camp entrance, I felt like a walking block of ice. It was mid-afternoon and still light out, but the camp was brighter than daylight. It took me a moment to realize that flames dotted numerous points in the camp. A bomb had hit here too?

Juli ran to our straggling group as we passed the gates, "You're safe!" she cried. "I can hardly believe it." She wrapped one arm around me and another around Zenia.

"The camp was bombed as well?" I asked.

Juli nodded. "Your barracks was demolished. Thank goodness it was empty at the time."

"What else was hit?"

"The laundry," said Juli. "Inge is dead."

I felt a lurch of sadness in my heart. Inge had sometimes been kind.

"The officers' mess was also hit," said Juli. "But none of the officers was killed."

Terrible as it may sound, deep down I wished that the mess could have been hit during mealtime. It would have given me great satisfaction if at least some officers had died while they were stuffing their faces. As we walked past the flaming mass of wood that had been the officers' *Kantine*, a slave dashed out of the burning building, his hair smoking and a bundle cradled in his arms. I heard the crack of a rifle shot. The man fell, scattering the items he had been holding — half a ham and a few raw eggs. I looked in the direction that the shot had come from.

Officer Schmidt glared at us and cocked his rifle. "I'd think twice about looting," he said.

All that food going up in flames while people were starving. It seemed obscene.

Juli led us to the hospital. "I'm going to give you first aid myself," she said. "The doctor and nurses have fled."

She ushered us into a room that was so crowded with wounded labourers that there was barely room on the floor for us to sit, but I was thankful nonetheless. All those people meant the room was warm.

Juli brought over a basin of water and a bottle of disinfectant. She cleaned surface scratches on my face and scalp that I didn't even know I had, then she gingerly removed my thin shoes and washed my feet with warm water and disinfectant. As they thawed out, I could feel sharp needles of pain on the soles of my feet, my ankles and in the joints of my toes. My feet were puffy and red, but at least now they were warming up. When she was finished, she took a clean white bedsheet and tore it into strips. "Wrap your feet in this before you put your shoes back on," she said.

"You're going to get in trouble," I said, taking the strips from her and holding them to my face. They were soft and warm and they smelled of soap, not bleach.

"The Nazis are fleeing," said Juli. "I've heard whispers that the Front is close. We'll need to get out of here or there will be fighting right on top of us, but right now you should rest and get your strength up."

She cleaned and disinfected Zenia's scratches, then wrapped Kataryna's ankle and worked on Natalia. The three girls cuddled up together and were soon fast asleep.

My feet had been sore and swollen for so long that even loose strips of cloth felt agonizingly tight and I couldn't sleep. I sat up and looked around me. So many of us and we were all in danger.

With half-opened eyes, I watched Juli tend each new person who tumbled in to the treatment room and collapsed on the floor. I marvelled at her stamina and her compassion. I also wondered about who was left guarding us at the camp. Most of the Nazis had fled, Juli said, but Officer Schmidt was still out there. I could still hear the occasional *pop pop pop*. Was he shooting people at random?

When Juli was finished treating everyone, I thought she would lie down and get some needed rest, but she left the room. I tried to stand up but the rags were too tight, so I unwrapped the cotton from my feet, slipped on my shoes, then followed Juli down the hallway without her noticing me. She stepped into a small back office at the very end. I remembered this room as the one that the nurses and doctor had used. When she came out, she was holding a pistol and she had a determined expression on her face. She looked up and gasped in surprise when she saw me standing there.

"What are you doing with that gun?"

"What needs to be done."

She spun the ammunition cylinder. "It's loaded."

"When did you learn about guns?"

Her eyes met mine. "There are many skills I have that you don't know about."

She walked down the hallway, passing me without so much as a pause, and walked out the front door.

"Juli. Don't — "

She flicked her hand at me dismissively and strode quickly, gun in full view at her side, to the open area of the camp.

I tried to keep up with her, but my sore feet slowed me down. I got to the far end of the open area and leaned against the corner of a building. My heart was in my mouth as I watched Juli keep walking.

Officer Schmidt strutted out of one of the still-standing buildings on the other side of the grounds, rifle at his side. His eyes went from Juli's face to the pistol in her hand. A wave of shock passed over his face. "Put the gun down, girl."

"I don't take orders from you anymore," said Juli. She pointed the pistol at his head.

Officer Schmidt's eyes widened in surprise. "Oh, you'll obey me. Put it down now."

He raised his rifle. In a flash Juli aimed the pistol and pulled the trigger. A loud bang cracked through the air.

Officer Schmidt jerked back. He stumbled a little bit, and tried to regain his balance. A patch of slick wet marked his uniform just below the shoulder.

Juli wasted no time. She pulled the trigger again. This time she missed him by a long way. I saw a spiral of smoke some distance behind him where the bullet hit the ground.

Officer Schmidt smiled. With cruel deliberation, he aimed at Juli and squeezed the trigger. At that very moment, I heard a double *boom*. Juli and Officer Schmidt both fell to the ground. This time I could see blood on his cheek. I ran to Juli. A blossom of red stained the waistband of her white smock. Her eyes locked on mine and she smiled. "You're safe now. Get out of here." Her eyes went dim.

"Juli, please wake up!" I fell to her side and tried to gather her in my arms, but her muscles were slack and she felt surprisingly heavy. That's how I knew she was dead. I gently closed her eyes with my fingertips, and scrabbled in the snow for a handful of dirt. I couldn't bury her, but I could not leave her here without a prayer for the dead. I sprinkled the dirt over her body and prayed the words I knew all too well.

My heart was filled with so much sadness, but I knew I had to act quickly. Juli had sacrificed her life so we could escape, and I owed it to her to try. I kissed her forehead. "Thank you, Juli. You are braver than anyone I can imagine."

I got up onto my feet and stumbled back to the hospital as quickly as I could, dark thoughts weighing me down. On the day that I discovered that my real sister might now be a Nazi, I had lost Juli, the sister of my heart.

I opened the hospital door and stepped into the corridor, the warmth enveloping me like a blanket. I heard alarmed murmuring from the treatment room. Juli was no longer there to help the wounded. I would escape, but first I needed to help any that I could. And Zenia. Would she escape with me? What about Kataryna and Natalia? I had to find out.

I stepped into the treatment room.

"Over to that side," said a boy wearing a Hitler Youth arm band, holding a rifle that dwarfed him. He pointed the barrel right at me.

Chapter Sixteen

Lace Curtain

The corner that he ordered me to was crowded by slave labourers who hadn't been injured too seriously. A boy wearing a man's Wehrmacht uniform stood at the other side of the room, hovering over the severely wounded.

Zenia was not in my group. Nor was Kataryna or Natalia. I scanned the wounded group, but they weren't there either. Where had they gone?

"All of you, out of the building," said the boy with the rifle. "And I don't want any trouble."

At gunpoint we marched in a scraggly single file towards the entrance of the camp, our way punctuated by burning buildings belching out smoke, and with the bodies of workers who had been shot for trying to plunder or escape. When we passed Juli's body, the girl behind me gasped, then let out one long sob. Officer Schmidt's body had already been removed and we passed that spot in silence. All that was left to show where he'd died was a splotch of blood in the muddy snow.

A canvas-covered military truck idled at the front entrance. "In," said the boy. "Make it fast."

I squeezed into a spot on the floor in the far back corner of the truck bed. The dozen of us were sardined so tightly that I had to hold my knees to my chest. It was impossible to protect myself from being bumped, but each time it happened, the person who bumped me would look up with forlorn eyes and apologize. I knew I wasn't the only one who was hurting.

Once the truck began to move, the canvas covering flapped in the wind, letting in the chilly winter air, but also letting us see the night sky. Against the black were darker silhouettes of planes. I knew they were dropping bombs. The countryside was unnaturally light with smoke and licking flames. I could see the worried faces of my fellow prisoners illuminated. I asked no one in particular, "What's going on?"

A man in the far shadows said, "They're taking us to another work camp."

A toothless woman who looked vaguely familiar scrutinized my face. "Aren't you Lida, the girl who sews?"

I nodded.

She pulled something from around her neck and handed it to me.

My crucifix.

"Where did you get this?"

"Your friend gave it to me just before she and two other young girls escaped."

My heart felt like it had stopped beating.

The woman grinned. "Oh yes, dear. A dozen or so got out. Mostly men, but also those three girls. They managed to sneak out just before those stupid boys dressed as Nazis showed up. Your friends were frantic to find you, but they couldn't wait any longer. The one girl took her crucifix off and asked me if I would give it to you if I ever saw you again." She touched my cheek. "Didn't think I would, but here you are."

I slipped the necklace over my head and felt the warmth of the cross against my chest. My friends had escaped! Please, please be safe! This crucifix had kept Zenia safe all these months and now she was wishing that safety to me.

This bit of metal was a link to my past and a talisman of good luck for the future. I held my hand over the cross and closed my eyes. Tato had made the strap out of shoe leather, but the crucifix itself was ancient. It had been passed down from eldest child to eldest child in our family for generations. Having it around my neck again made me feel that those spirits of past generations were watching over me, giving me strength. Much as I would have liked to curl up and die, it wasn't my right to do so. I was the oldest person left in our family, and it was my responsibility to find Larissa. It shamed me to think that just hours ago I had questioned her method of staying alive. Who was I to judge her? Hadn't the Nazis taken me as well? We were all cogs in their evil machinery, even those young boys dressed up as soldiers.

"Why are they moving us?" I asked the woman.

"The Front is just a few miles away," she said. "I don't suppose they're trying to save us. They likely just need slaves deeper inside the Reich."

✦ ✦ ✦

I slept fitfully to the smell of diesel, sweat and disinfectant. I dreamed of a blond girl dressed in pink. Her eyes were round with fear and her hands reached out to me. "Save me, Lida!" she screamed.

I woke up with such a jolt it took me a few minutes to remember where I was. The army truck bumped and swerved across rough, bombed-out, pothole-filled roads, throwing those of us in the back painfully against each other. How long had we been travelling? Hours, I was certain, not days. The bomb at the factory had blasted the soup out of my hands, so the last time I had eaten had been the sawdust bread at breakfast. I should have been hungry, but I was beyond that. Had I eaten since then, I might have thrown it up.

When the truck finally stopped, daylight poured down through the openings in the canvas flaps, showing the Allied bomber planes in stark relief against the blue sky. The back of the truck opened with a loud screech and clunk.

"Out. All of you. Now," a Nazi policeman ordered, his rubber truncheon raised threateningly.

I stumbled out on numb feet and nearly fell to the ground, but by sheer force of will I stayed upright. I reached out and grabbed the toothless woman's arm so she could lean on me as she got out. We all needed to look healthier than we were. It could mean the difference between a work camp or a shot to the head.

I looked around, trying to figure out where we might be. We were at the edge of a village or town. Tidy timber-framed cottages lined either side of a cobblestone road, and a squat stone church sat just beyond, surrounded by an old graveyard. The mountain range in the distance made the scene seem almost idyllic. Was this a place that had not been touched by war?

But once the policeman ordered us to walk, I began to notice the familiar pockmarks on the sides of houses and on the road — those could only have got there with repeated bombings, yet the houses still stood. Ice-slicked cobblestones were a challenge, but I balanced as best I could, praying that I wouldn't twist an ankle.

As we walked, I noticed movement behind a lace curtain in the window of one cottage. The lace was pulled back and a rosy-cheeked housewife stared out at us. I met her eye briefly, then the curtain abruptly closed. What was she thinking? Perhaps it was an everyday occurrence for her — emaciated slaves being marched down the middle of her street. Perhaps she didn't think about it at all anymore.

At the end of the street was a low stone structure built into the side of a hill. It looked as if it might have been a large horse stable at one time, or maybe an old factory. Three of the four walls were built into the rise of the hill. The toothless old woman, perhaps seeing that I looked puzzled, said that such places were attractive to the Nazis. After all the Allied bombings they had endured, they sought out structures like this that had natural defenses.

The policeman stepped up to the door of an ancient cottage beside the building and banged on it. We twelve tired workers stood on the cold cobblestones and waited, wondering what fate had in store for us now.

A civilian with a moustache opened the door. I could smell the steam of food from inside — sharp cheese, onions, fried eggs? My stomach lurched in hunger.

The policeman said, "I have your workers."

The man didn't bother getting a coat or jacket. In his white shirtsleeves, he stepped out and inspected us, one by one. "Hold out your hands," he said to me.

I did.

"This one is fine."

He examined each of us the same way, and passed us all until he got to the toothless woman. When she held out her gnarled fingers, he flicked his hand like he was brushing away a fly. "Too old."

"I'm not," said the woman. "I am a good worker. Stronger than I look."

The policeman took her roughly by the arm. "I'll get rid of her," he said to the man.

I knew that the woman was not that old at all. When you're fed nothing but turnip soup and bread made of sawdust, it is hard to keep up your strength. My guess was that she was no older than that housewife who had watched us through the lace curtains.

As she was led away, I wondered if the housewife would watch and judge.

The man walked along the front of the low building and directed those of us deemed suitable to follow him. The far end of the building looked like it had sunk into the earth from the weight of the hill behind it. There was a set of stone steps leading down to what looked like a wide root-cellar door. He went down the steps and opened it.

"This is where you'll be," he said, waving us in with his hand.

The smell of misery hit me first. It was one that I was all too familiar with: a combination of unwashed bodies, no fresh air and bad food. It took my eyes some time to become adjusted to the dim light, but as shapes emerged, I realized that I was standing in some sort of machine room. There were individual presses and sanders like I had seen at the metalworks factory, but these seemed not so modern. As my eyes got more used to the dimness, I noticed filthy straw mattresses lined up against the walls. I could smell the open barrel in the corner before I saw it.

We weren't the first people to work in this hidden place, but I hoped we would be the last. What had happened to the ones who had been here before us? By the smell of the room, they weren't long gone.

"You will sleep here," the man said, pointing to the mattresses. "That is your toilet." His hand indicated the open barrel. "Food will be brought in twice a day."

He walked over to a long table and picked up a shiny metal cylinder that looked like an oversized bullet. "This is what we're making here."

It was like a nightmare repeating itself. He showed us in great detail the steps involved in making the ammunition. My assignment — again — was measuring out the gunpowder. Only this time I was tamping it into small cartridges instead of bombs.

"I inspect every cartridge each night," said the man. "If I find any defective cartridges, one of you will be chosen at random to be shot."

I looked around at the ten others who shared my fate. I was the youngest by far. We were a sorry group of starving, broken ghosts. How many of us would survive long enough for the war to end? My hand went up to the crucifix around my neck. This man had not asked us to remove any metal. He didn't seem to care if we were all killed in one big blast. I was glad to have my crucifix with me. It made me feel protected by the spirits of my family. And if there was a spark? So be it.

❖ ❖ ❖

How long did we stay in that prison? Time blended into one long nightmare. Not once were we allowed to leave the building. At night as we lay on the lice-infested mattresses that had been used by many slaves before us, I tried to get the others to sing, but they were too tired. The only things that sustained me were my hopes and dreams. No one could take those away from me.

Day after day, when the man came in, the scents that clung to him were my only calendar. I inhaled the humid leaves of autumn, then drank the dry bouquet of fresh snow. Slush came next. Was winter nearly over? I waited for the scent of lilacs, but it never came. Only mud.

I dreamed of little Larissa often. In time, that horrible image of the girl who looked like her in that Nazi car faded from my memory. Instead I thought of earlier times — especially that one time when she sat on my shoulders in the spring so she could reach the tallest blooms of our lilac tree. I willed the heady memory of lilac perfume to replace the odour of oppression. I thought of the friends I had met since I had been captured — Luka and Zenia, Natalia and Kataryna. I hoped that they were safe. I longed to see them again, even once, just to know that they had survived. I prayed for Juli's soul and I felt guilty that she'd died for my freedom, yet I was still a captive. I hoped that somehow I would make her proud of me.

Chapter Seventeen

Shokolad

How I hated that man who came each day and took away the cartridges and brought us our slop. But then one day he didn't come. Or the next day. Now that he wasn't showing up, I was aware of his absence. He was our only link to the outside.

We had made all the cartridges that we could but we ran out of gunpowder and cylinders. There were so many cartridges that they filled the box and we had to stack the overflow on the table, but they kept rolling off.

We had no food.

My body had become used to living on our meagre diet, but to survive on nothing was not possible. Each day, every day had been punctuated with that piece of sawdust bread and that bowl of turnip soup. Even with that food, my arms and legs had turned to sticks and my teeth had loosened. Now my feet stank from their open wounds and my knees buckled when I tried to stand. I lay on my lice-infested mat and waited to die, hoping that somehow my sister would live. I lost all track of time.

✤ ✤ ✤

The floor shook.

Bits of stone crumbled from the earthen wall and hit me on the cheek. A bomb? Was this how I would finally die? I turned my face to the wall and closed my eyes.

A loud pounding on the door. I pushed myself up to a sitting position.

The wood cracked. People around me roused and stumbled to their feet. Someone pulled on my arm and I got up too, although the pressure of the cold stone floor on the sores of my feet was nearly unbearable.

We clustered at the back of the room, our arms wrapped around each other so the weakest wouldn't fall, huddled in fear.

Bang . . . bang . . . bang . . . Soon the door was nothing but splinters. With one final loud smash of a booted foot hitting the wood, what was left of the door fell away. A gust of fresh air brushed against my face. I breathed in the incredible sweetness. It had been so long since I had smelled fresh air.

A soldier stepped through the splinters of wood.

But it wasn't a Nazi. He had no arm band where the swastika should have been. And his helmet was bowl-shaped, not curving out at the edges. He blinked a few times, as if he couldn't quite comprehend who or what we were. He reached for his pocket. Was there a gun in there? But no, he took out a handkerchief and held it to his face. That embarrassed me. I knew we stank. Would he think we were pigs like the Nazis did?

He said something in a language that I didn't under-stand, but a rheumy-eyed prisoner with rags on his feet perked up at the words. He answered in the same language, then translated for us.

"He's an American soldier. The Nazis are losing on all fronts. He will give us food, and he will get us medical treatment."

I tried cheering, but I was so weak that it came out like the croak of a frog. I could feel my eyes tickling with the thought of tears, but I was too thirsty to weep. Was it really over? Could I now find my sister and go home?

The soldier asked another question and the prisoner translated for us. "He wants to know how many of us can walk out and how many need to be carried. He can get stretchers."

We were all weak and hungry and every one of us had trouble standing, but we decided as a group that we would walk out with our dignity. It was our victory after all. We looped our arms around one another and stepped out of that horrible building and into the light.

The sunlight felt like a knife to my tender eyes. I covered my face with my hands so just a bit of the sun could shine through. I felt a warm hand on my shoulder as I listened to gentle murmuring in that strange language. The voice guided me somewhere and I followed him without hesitation. Everything about his manner showed that he considered me human — equal to him. I didn't have to understand the words to know that I could trust him.

Soon I found myself sitting on a bench, and when I could finally take my hands away from my face, I saw that the soldier was sitting beside me, watching me with concern. He held a metal flask.

"Drink."

He tipped it up to his own mouth to demonstrate, then handed it to me.

I lifted it gingerly to my parched lips and felt the cool clean water moisten my swollen tongue. I swallowed, nearly choking, then sipped some more. It tasted so good.

The soldier rooted around in the pocket of his trousers and pulled out a small metallic packet. He set it on my open palm.

"Eat," he said, motioning with his hands and pointing to his mouth. "Chocolate."

Shokolad?

I knew that word. I looked down at the small package. It did not look like what I knew as *shokolad.*

He took it from me and bit into a corner of the metal, ripping off a bit of the package and opening it up. He shook out a small brown square and handed it back to me.

I held it to my nose and sniffed. It smelled heavenly. It was nothing like the sweet from the Nazi Brown Sister. Could it really be *shokolad?* I had only tasted it once as a very young child, but this scent brought the memory back.

I tried to bite into it but it was too firm for my wobbly teeth. The soldier took it from me again and broke off a small corner. I put that bit in my mouth and held it on my tongue. An explosion of flavour filled my mouth as that small morsel of chocolate slowly dissolved. I closed my eyes and savoured it.

I wanted to eat more but the soldier shook his head. He slipped the chocolate back into its metallic package and placed it in my palm, folding my fingers around it. I understood that he was giving it to me but didn't want me to eat it all at once. I slipped it into my pocket.

My eyes had gradually adjusted to the light so I took a look around me. The bench where I sat was on that cobblestone street of quaint cottages. Army trucks with a white star emblazoned on the wood idled all along it. There was even a tank. American soldiers, all looking impossibly tall with clean hair and all their teeth, were busy setting up tents and chatting in clusters. I looked across the road and noticed the blue-shuttered cottage. That same ruddy-cheeked woman stared out through her lace curtains. Her eyes darted fearfully from me to the soldier at my side. The sight of her made me unbearably angry. All this time we had been starving, locked up mere steps from her house. Had she thought of us once? And now she was afraid.

The soldier followed my gaze. He stood up and motioned for me to come with him. He held my elbow as we walked to that house and he banged on the door. The woman disappeared from the window but she didn't answer. He banged again. No response. He kicked it hard with his boot and the door flew open. We stepped inside.

A portrait of Hitler over the fireplace draped with black ribbon. Underneath, a picture of a young man in uniform, a black ribbon of mourning around it as well. Threadbare furniture, meticulously clean. The woman cowered in the archway between the living room and her kitchen, her eyes cast down.

The soldier gestured for me to come in and look around, but somehow now that we were face to face, I couldn't bear to hate that woman. Was that a picture of her son? Had he died, fighting for Hitler? Was Hitler now dead as well?

Then the woman met my eyes and said in German. "Take what you want."

I followed her into the kitchen. She opened up one cupboard after another, showing me how little she had. Mostly jars of pickled vegetables. Her most precious item was a stale loaf of dark bread and my mouth watered at the sight of it, but how could I take it from this woman who had so little?

She cut off a thick slice and handed it to me. I thanked her in German and held it to my face, breathing in the wonderful aroma of yeast and rye. How long had it been since I had held a piece of bread that was not made of sawdust? I longed to eat it, but my stomach was still roiling from that tiny piece of rich chocolate. Now that I finally had food, I couldn't eat it. I put the slice of bread in my pocket, feeling more secure just knowing it was there.

When we walked out of her house, I saw that the rest of the soldiers had bashed open other houses. Mostly what the slaves carried out were bits of food, like a small wedge of cheese or a jar of pickled herring, but some brought out looted treasures that Nazi soldiers at the Front must have sent home to their families.

The man who had translated for the soldier cradled a large wooden icon of the Madonna in his arms. He was so weak that it took all his strength to hold onto it, but I could see the determination on his face. A soldier stepped in to help him with it. The sight of the plundered painting made me want to cry. It looked so much like the ancient icon that had been stolen from my blue-painted church back home. I watched as a soldier found the man a blanket to wrap the icon in. They loaded it carefully into the back of an army Jeep.

I walked over to the man and silently stood beside him as we watched the Jeep drive away.

"Where are they taking it?" I asked him.

"There is a Ukrainian Catholic priest in a refugee camp nearby who is building a temporary church for us," he said. "The icon is a start."

I reached into my pocket and pulled out my piece of bread. I tore it in half and gave one piece to him. He held it to his lips but did not eat it.

Chapter Eighteen

Looking for Larissa

It was a nurse who took Larissa away from me, and it was the doctor at the work camp who killed children for their blood. When the Americans took me to their hospital, I couldn't stop screaming.

They took away my blue flannel dress. I was channelled into a lineup, naked and shivering, for a shower. I refused to go in.

A nurse picked me up and carried me in, ignoring my screams and scratches — ignoring the hot water that streamed down her uniform and ruined her leather shoes. When the warm water coursed through my hair and over my face, my muscles relaxed and I clung to that nurse as if she were my mother. Soaking wet and fully dressed, she sat me on her lap and rocked me, cooing a lullaby as she gently massaged shampoo into my hair and lovingly soaped away the months of dirt encrusted beneath my fingernails and behind my ears. I sobbed when she lathered the soap with her fingertips and gently massaged the soft suds into the wounds on my feet and legs. She washed sores I didn't even know I had on my back and on my elbows. It had been so long since someone had cared for me that I could barely stand it.

The soap she used smelled like lilacs. It was nothing like that bleaching powder. She used real shampoo for my hair, so my scalp didn't sting a bit. She wrapped me in a towel and she dried herself as well. Her nurse's cap was wilted and ruined and her bun had come unpinned.

When I was dry, she gave me back my blue flannel dress. As I pulled it over my head, I wrinkled my nose at the unmistakable chemical smell of lice-killer. I longed for a future when that poison was no longer necessary.

Once I was clean, I thought she would let me go to one of the camps for refugees. I wanted to go to the one with the priest and the makeshift church with the icon of the Virgin Mary, but Nurse Astrid said not yet. She brought me to a long corridor of white beds that were not made of filthy straw. Each bed held a slave labourer who had been injured in a different way. Bandages covering eyes, or a leg in a cast suspended by a pulley. Some looked whole, but they stared at the ceiling without blinking. She lifted me onto an empty bed at the end of the corridor.

When she held a syringe to my arm, I tried to pull away. My mind knew that Nurse Astrid was trying to heal me, but my heart remembered the terrible things that had happened to children in that hospital in the work camp. "Please trust me," she said in American-accented Ukrainian.

I took a deep breath and closed my eyes. I tried to trust her.

She brought a doctor who did things to my feet and legs

that hurt beyond belief. When I tried to crawl away, Astrid was the one who caught me and threatened to tie me to the bed. "Please trust me," she said.

Astrid fed me. First just spoonfuls, and as my stomach got stronger, mouthfuls. My hunger roared like a lion. I could have eaten non-stop if she'd let me.

I knew that Astrid was being kind, but everything she did reminded me that I was still a prisoner. More than anything I wanted to get away. To begin my search for Larissa and for us to both go home.

When my feet had no more open wounds, Astrid would come by with a salve and massage them. It hurt intensely when she did it, but I also knew it was good for my feet.

"Soon you'll be ready to leave," she said.

One morning after breakfast she placed a big wrinkled paper bag beside me on my hospital bed and grinned. "Open it."

Inside was a pair of thick woollen socks and a pair of sturdy leather boots that looked to be my size. My eyes filled with tears. The shoes that Juli had given me were so badly worn that they had disintegrated long ago. Clothing was scarce with all the refugees to be cared for, and footwear was even harder to come by, yet Astrid had somehow found me these precious items.

"Thank you," I said in her language. It was one of the first phrases of English that I had learned.

It was early June and warm out, but the wool felt good on my feet. I laced the boots up as tightly as I dared and took a few steps. Slowly I was beginning to feel like a human again.

It struck me that Astrid looked so much like that nurse who had taken Larissa away from me, and it made me wonder. Did that other nurse think she was somehow healing us with her actions? I would probably never know.

Astrid got permission to take me by Jeep to the displaced persons' camp with the makeshift church. The distance between the hospital and the camp was not great, but it took several hours because the roads were clogged with ragged refugees. They would travel in clusters but not all in the same direction.

"They go from camp to camp, looking for loved ones," said Astrid.

I searched the faces as we passed them, and I looked especially carefully whenever I saw a girl with blond hair, but I never saw anyone who could be Larissa. The refugees were a wild assortment, speaking more languages than I ever knew existed. Some pushed wheelbarrows piled high with plundered china plates. Others, carrying battered suitcases overflowing with yellowed family photos, looked too healthy to be refugees. More than a few were clothed in striped rags. Gaunt beings clutched a piece of bread or a jar of pickles as if it were the finest treasure on earth.

The countryside was pocked with ragged craters where bombs had landed and it was rare to see a building standing. The road itself was a maze of rubble and holes, and I knew that unexploded land mines littered the ground, but Astrid manoeuvred like an expert.

"Here we are," she said, pulling up to the one standing section of an ancient stone wall. Hundreds of bits of paper fluttered from it, their corners shoved into the crevices and cracks to secure them. "This used to be a convent."

The sight of those hundreds of papers made me panic. By the time my father had been taken by the Soviets, praying was against the law. I had watched my mother fold up a note in the middle of the night and walk in the cover of darkness to our little blue church. It had been locked, and the priest executed, so what was she doing there? The next day I had crept to the church when no one was looking. I found her note tucked into a crack in the church wall. I pulled it out and read her plea to God to bring my father home. Then I took the note and placed it on my tongue, swallowing it like a sacrament. I wanted my father home too, but didn't my mother realize she risked all our lives by writing that note? I never told her what I had done.

Astrid took my hand and together we walked over to those fluttering bits of prayer. I reached up and held one flat so I could read it. *Anya Zuk, from Drohobych, looking for Ivan. Left for Flensburg June 2, 1945.* I looked at another, and another. All were details of refugees, searching for their loved ones.

"Will they get into trouble for making these notes?" I asked.

Astrid shook her head. "Who is it you're looking for, Lida? I'll help you go through these."

I told her about Larissa, but also about Luka and Zenia, Kataryna and Natalia. My heart ached as I read the details of so many lost loved ones, but I kept my hope until the very last paper. When we were finally done and I found no one I loved, I wanted to curl up and weep, but Astrid told me she would send my name and the names of my dear ones to the Red Cross.

"It may take time," she said. "But maybe we will find someone you know."

With her hand draped lightly across my shoulder, she led me inside the refugee camp.

Chapter Nineteen

Praying for Larissa

The smell of bleaching powder but not misery. No barbed wire. No Nazi soldiers with guns. This refugee camp had taken on a personality while I was being treated at the hospital. Fragments of families had claimed corners of rooms in the various blasted-out convent buildings. Others had built makeshift homes amidst the rubble from what they could find — twisted metal, broken-down doors, half-bricks.

The first thing I looked for was the church. People grinned when I asked about it and pointed me to an area at the back of the camp. Set off to one side was what looked like a long-abandoned barn on the outside, but there was a well-trod path leading up to it. I walked to the door and it creaked loudly as I opened it.

Sunlight poured in from the shattered rafters.

I gasped in amazement at what I saw. An altar neatly made of stacked tin cans with a wooden door laid across as a tabletop. The stolen icon from that German house

was propped up in the centre of the altar, a golden can-
delabra on one side and dirt-filled tin cans holding hand-
dipped candles on the other side. On the back wall of the
barn hung a handmade wooden cross.

I knelt down before the altar and sobbed a prayer for
the souls of my mother, father, grandmother. I hoped that
soon they could rest in peace.

I was safe.

I would find Larissa.

I said a prayer of thanks that I still lived, and then
another of hope, for Luka . . . Zenia . . . Kataryna . . . Mary
. . . Natalia . . .

Larissa.

I don't know how long I stayed in contemplation, but it
must have been quite a while. When I tried to stand up, I
couldn't. My legs and feet were stiff and numb.

"Let me help you."

A voice from a distant dream. I looked up.

The way the light shone through the broken slats in the
barn roof made it difficult to see who was standing there,
but the silhouette was beloved. The voice was dear. Could
it possibly be?

"Luka?"

He stepped forward. His shock of wild hair had grown
back but his eyes were circled with shadows of grief.
"They told me I might find you here." He knelt and
placed my arms around his neck.

Together we stood. "Dear Lida," he said. "I promised I
would find you."

"I dreamt of you the night you escaped."

He smiled. "I was thinking of you as well, praying that

you would be safe. I felt guilty leaving you behind."

"How did you manage to get away?"

We walked out of the makeshift church together — Luka still helping me, although my feet and legs were feeling less numb — and he told me about that night.

"I couldn't just walk out," he said. "During the day there were too many people around, and at night the gates were locked and guards with guns were on patrol."

"So how did you escape?"

"Did you ever see what they did with the dead bodies?" he asked.

I shuddered at the memory. "They piled them into trucks."

Luka nodded. "There were many trucks. Many deaths at the hospital. I got out on one of those trucks."

I looked at Luka, not sure that I had heard correctly. "You hid among the corpses?"

"Yes."

We walked in silence past children playing with makeshift toys, and mothers scrubbing rags in soapy basins of water. What a contrast to be with people smiling and relaxed when in my mind was the image of Luka in a truck of the dead.

"It must have been awful," I said.

He squeezed my hand and sighed. "I managed to loosen the tarp from the back of the truck and jump out onto the road when we were a good distance from the camp. Thank goodness it was dark out. I hid in the woods and met up with others who had escaped from camps as well."

"You stayed in the woods all that time?"

He looked at me but his eyes seemed distant. "We

moved around a lot. The Nazis hunted us down. Not all our group survived."

We were each lost in our own thoughts and without realizing it, we reached the end of the refugee camp. I sat down on the tire of an abandoned Jeep and patted the spot beside me. Luka sat as well.

"When did you get here?" I asked.

"A day or so ago," he said. "I found out that a group of survivors from our work camp had been taken to the American army hospital down the road. I thought that if you were among that group, you would end up here."

"Have you found any others?"

Luka shook his head. "I haven't seen anyone else I knew from there."

❖ ❖ ❖

Luka and I spent as much time as we could together over the next days and weeks. There was much work to do — helping families patch together makeshift homes, assisting with food distribution, playing with the younger children. He was much healthier than most of the refugees, and now that my feet were healing and I was eating more than turnip soup, I had become stronger as well. Luka found a place to sleep with a group of boys his age. I found a cozy spot on my own in the corner of what used to be an office in one of the convent buildings.

Every morning I would check with the people from the Red Cross to see if there was any word about Larissa, but each day the answer was the same.

"I am sorry, dear," said the kind-hearted Canadian woman whose hair was a mass of red curls. "I hope we'll have better news for you soon."

"Is there any way of checking German records?"

"What do you mean?" asked the woman.

"I may have seen her with some Germans," I said evasively. I didn't want to admit that I thought I had seen her with a Nazi officer's family.

"The Germans destroyed records as they abandoned offices," said the woman, "but we're doing the best that we can."

Her words cut me to the heart. What chance did I really have of ever finding my sister? I didn't even know if she would be using her real name, if she'd been living with that Nazi family I saw in the car.

Later, when I sat beside Luka and we ate tasty buns made with white flour and a faint taste of sugar, he said, "Don't ever give up hope. All you can do is keep on looking. She's probably looking for you as well."

He was right, and I knew it. Every day I checked the fluttering messages, hoping that one day I would see a message from my sister.

Luka checked as well. He had no way of finding his father, who was either still in Siberia or dead by now. But his mother had been a slave labourer. Perhaps one day a fluttering message from her would appear.

Chapter Twenty

The Lucky Ones

Life in the displaced persons' camp settled into a routine. Each morning we children would be gathered together in a makeshift classroom to be taught Ukrainian and English spelling and grammar, arithmetic, history, geography. For so long I had pretended to be older than I was, and it was difficult for me to be clustered together with the other eleven-year-olds. Many of these children had lived through conditions as difficult as my own, but a few had managed to stay with a parent or grandparent throughout the war. These few lucky ones seemed so separate and special. Did I dare admit how jealous I was of them?

I knew it wasn't fair of me to feel that way, but every time I looked at the lucky ones, I felt unbearably lonely. I was grateful to be with Luka, but I had to find Larissa, and it wasn't just to ensure that she was safe. I needed to find her for my own sake. We were sisters, after all. We shared the same family, childhood — even thoughts. With her gone, half of me was gone as well.

My teacher was a former high school instructor from Lviv named Pani Zemluk and she was demanding and precise in her expectations. Often after all the other children had gone off to play, I would stay at my spot on the bench made from a plank of wood and two empty paint tins, my workbook open on my knees. I was determined to master my school work, especially the English language. It was such a gift to finally be given the opportunity to learn. Pani Zemluk would come and sit beside me, correcting my errors and giving me extra exercises when I wanted them. And we would talk.

I confided to her my hopes and dreams of finding Larissa. I confessed to her what I did in the war. I wept on her shoulder as I admitted to accepting the candy from that Nazi woman, and how my selfishness had destroyed my family.

"It's not your fault," she said. "What starving child would say no to a sweet? It was meant to be."

Pani Zemluk advised me to change my identity. "You cannot let people know that you're from Chernivets'ka. That's in the Soviet part of Ukraine, and everyone from there is being sent back to the Soviet Union."

"But I want to go home."

"Your home no longer exists. Besides, you were a labourer for the Nazis. If you go back to the Soviet Union, you will be punished for that."

I rubbed the tears away with the back of my hand and stared at her. "That makes no sense," I said. "I was a *prisoner* of the Nazis."

"No matter. You will be punished as a Nazi."

"They already know my true identity at the hospital," I

told her. "Besides, if I change who I am, how can I ever find my sister?"

Pani Zemluk brushed away a stray hair from my brow and looked me in the eye. "Your first job is to save yourself, Lida. You have been very lucky so far, but if you don't stay free, you and your sister can never hope to be reunited."

Her words shattered me.

Luka was in the spiralling lineup of refugees at lunchtime. Once we each got a brimming bowl of hot pea soup and a handful of crackers, we walked down the pathway to the makeshift church. It was cool there, and quiet at midday. We sat side by side on the ground, leaning against the wall.

I filled my spoon with thick soup and blew on it, waiting for it to cool down just a bit. I didn't actually like the taste of pea soup — we'd been served it more than any other food — but it filled my stomach and staved off the gnawing hunger that seemed always to be present. I swallowed down the first spoonful, then as I waited for the next to cool, I watched Luka. He shovelled down the soup, piping hot. The look on his face was one of urgency, as if he was afraid that someone would take the food away from him if he didn't consume every last speck instantly.

"Have you heard anything about your mother?" I asked him.

He shook his head and continued eating. I swallowed down another spoonful of soup, then as I stared at my bowl, I told Luka about what Pani Zemluk had said.

Luka didn't answer right away. He was too involved with licking every last bit of soup from the bottom of his bowl. When he was finished, he methodically ate his crackers, chewing each one with gusto. Once he swallowed down the last cracker he turned to me and said, "I think she is wrong."

His words confused me. "So you think we should go back to the Soviet Union?"

"I haven't heard anything about my mother," said Luka. "But this morning some Red Army soldiers came into my classroom and asked to speak to me."

His words made my heart pound. "What did they want?"

"They told me that my father is alive and that he is living in Kyiv. He's got his own pharmacy."

"That is wonderful, Luka!"

"They are coming back tomorrow morning. They will take me home."

His words were like a stone in my heart. I had no idea if I would ever find Larissa, but Luka was right here, with me. He was the brother of my heart. How could I bear to lose him yet again? Was I destined to be all alone? I didn't say anything. I stared at the soup in my bowl, but suddenly I had no appetite.

Luka's finger gently brushed a tear away from my cheek. "You could come with me," he said.

Should I? Could I? But if I went back to the Soviet Union and Larissa was living somewhere here in Germany, how would I ever find her? It was all too overwhelming. There was too much to think about.

"I am leaving tomorrow morning, no matter what," said Luka. "Come and say goodbye to me, or come and join me. Your choice."

Chapter Twenty-One

Luka Leaving

All night I tossed and turned. How wonderful it would be to go home again and help rebuild all that had been lost. Maybe I could go to Kyiv with Luka. Maybe his father would adopt me and then I would truly be Luka's sister.

But what if Pani Zemluk was right?

Even if she was wrong, there was one thing I knew to be true. If I went with Luka now, I would never find Larissa. No place could be home without my sister.

I got up at dawn the next morning and found Luka. He had just a small cloth satchel with all his worldly goods — a prayer book that had been given to him by a priest, a notebook from his teacher and a second set of clothing. We walked together to the stone gate with its flutter prayers of paper, and waited for the Red Army truck.

We weren't the only ones waiting there. Three older men had congregated as well — two who had been slave labourers and one who had been a prisoner of war. It was a tired and sorry looking group. Pani Zemluk also came.

Her eyes widened in astonishment when she saw me standing beside Luka.

Just then the Red Army truck appeared at the end of the road. It approached slowly, spewing up billows of dust.

"Will you come with me?" asked Luka.

Pani Zemluk stepped forward and put her hand on my shoulder. "Lida, don't."

I studied her face. It was filled with concern and fear. I turned to Luka. His eyes looked serious, but he was hopeful as well.

I took a deep breath. It was now or never. "I cannot go with you."

He set his satchel down and wrapped his arms around me. "I wish you would come with me, but I understand why you can't come right now. Stay safe, sister of my heart," he said. "I will find a way to write to you when I meet my father in Kyiv. Maybe one day, you and your sister will join us."

"I would like that."

The canvas-covered truck pulled up just then and the sight of it made me panic. It looked so much like the truck that had transported me from the slave camp to my final prison. It could have been the same one, except where the swastika had been was a red star enclosing a hammer and sickle.

The truck careened to a stop in a swirl of dust and a fresh-faced Red Army officer stepped out. He took in the three older men and ticked off names on a clipboard. He approached me and Luka.

"You must be Luka Barukovich of Kyiv," he said in perfect Ukrainian to Luka. "But who are you?" He crouched down so his hazel eyes were level with mine. He smiled. "Are you coming home with us today?"

He seemed clean, friendly and relaxed. This soldier seemed nothing like those thugs who had taken my father. Maybe I had been wrong about all this. Maybe they had changed. How I longed to go with Luka. I dreaded being all alone, but I couldn't go just yet.

"I need to find my sister first."

"The Soviet Red Cross can help with that." He poised his pencil over his clipboard. "What is your sister's name and where were you two born?"

I opened my mouth to answer but was startled by a hand gripping my shoulder so tightly that it hurt. I looked up. Pani Zemluk's lips smiled but her eyes were serious. "Children should be seen and not heard."

I was about to protest, but noticed the anger that washed over the Red Army officer's expression as he put his pencil away. With his friendly mask down for just that brief moment, I'd had a glimpse of the bully behind it.

The teacher kept a tight grip on my shoulder, almost as if she had to keep me in that place.

I looked at Luka. "Please stay here with me."

"I must go back, Lida," he said, a touch of impatience in his voice. "My father is waiting for me."

With that, Luka tossed his rucksack into the back of the truck and climbed in under the canvas.

The other three joined Luka, and the officer got into the driver's seat and sped off. I walked out onto the street with Pani Zemluk at my side and watched them go, listening to the refrains of the Soviet national anthem from the back of the truck. When they were out of sight, Pani Zemluk loosened her grip on my shoulder.

"Never tell the Soviets who you really are."

I pointed to the fluttering bits of paper on the convent pillar. "Each of those gives a name and where the person is from."

Pani Zemluk nodded. "And the Soviets check those regularly."

I had much to think about as I walked back through the gates of the refugee camp. Luka was gone and I was all alone. I prayed that he would be all right, and I hoped that I had made the right decision in staying.

I passed a group of small children who were playing tag, screaming delightedly at each other as they darted through the legs of older refugees. No one seemed to mind. The sight of happy children had been all too rare these past years. Seeing those smiles made me think of Larissa. What would she be doing right now? If that really had been her in that car outside the bomb factory, she wouldn't be in a refugee camp. She would never put her name on a fluttering piece of paper. Wherever she was, I hoped she was safe.

I got my tin cup, spoon and bowl from my sleeping area and stood at the end of a snaking lineup of people who were waiting for breakfast. Each morning as I did this, it made me think of eating that horrible sawdust bread and coloured water for months on end. The food at this refugee camp was not tasty, but I never complained. It filled my stomach better than sawdust and turnip ever did.

In the weeks that I had been at the camp, hundreds more homeless people had poured in, yet the Americans had somehow provided food, and they scraped together bedding and soap as best they could. As I looked at the long column of people ahead of me, I noticed the ingenious variety of clothing that people had been able to patch together for themselves. A young girl up ahead wore the red of a Nazi flag as a kerchief for her hair and the man in front of me had patched his shirt with a paper memo about typhus. The woman behind me had woven a pair of sandals out of old newspapers. Many people wore remnants of Nazi uniforms — a jacket with the sleeves cut off, or trousers rolled up. But even with the insignia ripped off, the sight of that clothing sickened me.

When it was finally my turn for breakfast, I held up my bowl to the tired looking American private with a sheen of sweat on his brow. He dipped his ladle into the giant vat and swirled it. I watched as he filled my bowl to the brim with yet another bowl of thick pea soup. People who had been at this camp for a while hated this pea soup and had nicknamed it the green horror, but I could eat it every day and not complain. Anything but turnip. I carefully balanced my bowl and looked for a quiet place to eat. I ended up going back to the barn, wishing that Luka was with me. I sat down on the ground, leaning against the barn wall. From this vantage point, I could watch the activity of the refugee camp, but I was by myself. I dipped my spoon into the hot green mush and brought the first spoonful to my lips. I savoured every drop, closing my eyes and letting the thickness of the soup cover my tongue and coat my teeth before slowly swallowing it down. It felt so good to be filling my stomach with real food.

"Lida, can that possibly be you?"

I was jolted out of my reveries and nearly dropped my

bowl. My eyes flew open. There stood a girl just a bit older than me. Her hair was blond and silky clean and her cheeks were pink with a touch of sun. The voice was familiar, and the patch of dark blue flannel on her thread-bare dress meant that she had been in Barracks 7 at the work camp. All at once I realized who it was.

"Natalia?"

She nodded, grinning.

I carefully set my half-eaten bowl of soup on the ground and jumped up, wrapping my arms around her, making sure not to spill any of her soup either. We both knew how precious every drop of food was. She hugged me back and sat down beside me, our shoulders touching as we leaned against the barn and ate our breakfast in silence. Once we were finished, I asked her, "When did you get here?"

"Late last night."

"Where from?"

"I've been going from camp to camp, looking for my family," she said. "There was a group of us who arrived last night."

"Have you found any of your family?"

She shook her head.

"What about Kataryna and Zenia?"

"We escaped the work camp together and hid in the woods for weeks," she said. "But Kataryna was killed. She stepped on a land mine."

Poor Kataryna. My heart ached at the thought of her dead. "And Zenia?" I was almost afraid to ask.

"She and I hid in a few places, but mostly the root cellar of a bombed-out house until the spring. We survived on old potatoes and whatever else we could scrounge. We were picked up by the British together," said Natalia. "The British sorted the refugees, so she was taken to a Jewish camp and I was taken to one for Poles. I visited her a week ago and she seems happy, all things considered. They've got her working in the kitchen and she likes that."

I placed my hand over my crucifix and felt its warmth. Thank goodness Zenia was safe. She had lost so much already. I hoped that she would find a community in that camp.

"Have you heard anything about Luka?" asked Natalia.

"As a matter of fact, I have." I told her how he'd been at the camp for the last few weeks, and that he had just left before breakfast to go back to Kyiv. "They say his father is alive."

Natalia looked at me uneasily. "I hope for Luka's sake that they're telling him the truth."

Chapter Twenty-Two

Lost

I was so grateful that the day Luka had left for Kyiv, Natalia arrived. She sat in class with the older children after our breakfast, then we walked through the camp together, questioning the clusters and groups that we met up with to see if anyone had heard news about a friend or loved one. After supper we went to the fluttering messages and painstakingly read each one. By the time we were finished, Natalia was in tears. "So many people, all lost," she said. "How will the survivors ever find one another?"

"At least you found me," I said.

She smiled at that. "Yes, and I'm glad I did."

I told Natalia that she could share the small converted office space that I called my bedroom, so we walked to the supply area and an American issued her new blankets and a pillow. We stayed up late, talking about our lost friends and family, food we had been eating since the end of the war, food we'd love to eat again, things we would do when we finally found a home.

"Will you go back to Lviv?" I asked her.

"I haven't decided. If I can't find my parents, brother or sister, I will try to immigrate to Canada or the United States instead. Even if I find a relative, I hope they'd come with me rather than go back to Lviv."

I sat up in bed and stared at her. "But why wouldn't you want to go back to Lviv?"

"It's part of the Soviet Union now," said Natalia.

Her comment confused me. "But Pani Zemluk told me that I should tell the authorities I was born in Lviv. If Lviv is part of the Soviet Union now, what's the point of lying?"

"It's confusing," said Natalia. "But people like me and your teacher who were born in pre-war Poland are allowed to leave if they wish. People who were born in pre-war Soviet Ukraine don't have a choice. They're supposed to go back."

"So you would rather go to a country you know nothing about instead of your old home?"

"I will not live under Stalin," said Natalia. "Four years of Hitler was bad enough."

I lay back down on my bedroll and considered her words. Life was certainly not good under Stalin. It was bearable until my father was taken. I fell asleep, dreaming of a time when I was truly happy. When Tato was still alive, and Mama too. Larissa and me and the lilac tree . . .

That was all lost now.

❖ ❖ ❖

I woke in the middle of the night to cries for help. Natalia stayed deep in sleep. I didn't wake her, but slipped out of the little office bedroom and ran towards the shouting.

Through the darkness I saw silhouettes of refugees

down by the convent gate. I ran to them, weaving my way through the crowd. When I got to the front, Pani Zemluk was kneeling on the ground, cradling the limp body of a young man. His face and chest and arms glistened black with blood in the moonlight. Was this a refugee who had set out on his own and been attacked?

Pani Zemluk looked up and scanned the cluster of refugees, her eyes filled with urgency. "You," she said, pointing to one of the healthier looking men. "Help me carry him inside."

Pani Zemluk wrapped her arms around the uncon-scious young man's chest and gingerly lifted him up, mak-ing sure not to let his injured head fall back. The young refugee carefully gripped him by the knees and they car-ried him in past me.

It was Luka.

How could this be?

I followed them to the first-aid building and watched as they gently set Luka down on a cot, then Pani Zemluk turned on the light. Blood glistened on Luka's face. His clothing was torn, shredded at the knees, and his hands were covered with scrapes.

"Lida, get me a basin of water and some clean cloths," said Pani Zemluk.

I was grateful to be useful. Anything to help Luka. I filled a basin with water and found bandages and cloths in one of the cupboards. I brought these over to Pani Zem-luk and she gently wiped the blood away from Luka's face.

Most of the blood had come from a single scalp wound and once that was bandaged, he looked much more like himself. But what was he doing back here? And what had happened to him? A hundred questions swirled in my mind. Finally, thankfully, Luka opened his eyes. I could see fear and pain in them as his gaze met mine. He gripped my hand and tried to speak, but all that came out were racking sobs.

"Slowly," said Pani Zemluk. "Tell us what happened."

He gasped in a few deep breaths and after a while he found the strength to speak. "You were right, Lida. I should never have tried to go back."

I squeezed his hand.

"All was well for the first part of the trip," he went on. "The officer stopped when we were a few miles along the road and gave us kolbassa and cheese. We sang and laughed and talked about the war. He seemed sympathetic about my time as an Ostarbeiter."

"When did things change?" asked Pani Zemluk.

"He took us to a train depot at the border between the American and the Soviet zones. There were several dozen refugees who had been brought in from various camps — mostly men, but a few children and some younger women. As soon as we were out of view of the Americans, everything was different," said Luka. "No more food, no singing. Red Army soldiers punched and kicked me, then stole my boots and my satchel. They told me I would have no need for Western goods in the Siberian concentration camp they were taking me to."

"So they weren't taking you to Kyiv after all," said Pani Zemluk. It was a statement, not a question.

"They told me that my father had died a long time ago. They said I was a Nazi." Luka wept.

"But you were a *prisoner* of the Nazis!"

"That doesn't matter," said Luka. "They told me that anyone who was captured by the Nazis is considered a Nazi. Those who aren't executed are to be sent to 're-education' camps in Siberia."

Dozens of thoughts swirled through my mind. Natalia had been right, and so had Pani Zemluk. Luka couldn't go home after all, and neither could I. The fact that I had no choice did not make it simpler. In the back of my mind I had dreamed of going home some day. Going there with Larissa. I dreamed of finding our lilac tree together, maybe placing lilacs on our parents' graves. Now I knew I could never go back.

Mama always said beauty could be found anywhere, but where was the beauty in this situation? I looked at Luka, beaten and despairing. He'd lost his father today, but also his country. Most of all, he had lost his hope for the future.

"Luka," I said, gently squeezing his hand. "I am here. I will not leave you."

He was silent for a long time, but I could see the streams of tears coming from his closed eyes. I can only imagine the horrible thoughts he was having of his father's last days.

After a while the tears stopped and I thought he was asleep, but all at once his eyes opened and they locked onto mine. "Lida, I am so glad that you didn't come with me."

"How did you get away?"

"After I was beaten, some of the other men were lined up and shot. They shoved the rest of us into boxcars. We pried away one of the floorboards in our car," said Luka.

"Those of us who were strong enough lowered ourselves through that hole and dropped down onto the tracks. I'm not sure how many got away because we scattered in all directions in the darkness of night. By some miracle, I wasn't caught. The hardest part was getting past the Soviet police at the border to the American zone, but luck was on my side again because the border police got drunk. I waited until they fell asleep and crept back across to the American zone."

"Rest now," said Pani Zemluk. "You are safe."

Luka tried to sit up. "They may come back for me."

"Don't worry," said Pani Zemluk. "We will get you out of here."

I stayed by Luka's side for the remainder of that night, curled up on a chair but wide awake. When Luka cried out in his sleep, I would squeeze his hand to let him know that he was safe. But how safe were any of us? What had happened to Luka terrified me. Now I knew for certain that none of us could ever go home.

Chapter Twenty-Three

Fleeing

I patched the knees of Luka's trousers with the remnants of a shredded Nazi flag and darned the holes in his shirt with coarse thread from Pani Zemluk. How I wished the damage to his soul could be fixed that easily. We knew we could not stay in the American camp. The Soviets would be back, looking for him but also for me. I was sure that they suspected I was from the east, like Luka. We had one last bowl of pea soup and said goodbye to Natalia.

We joined the thousands of refugees who walked from camp to camp. There was safety in the crowds. If we weren't registered at a specific camp, how would the Soviets find us?

By August 1945, we had walked so many miles of dusty roads that my feet ached despite the good boots Astrid had given me. I despaired at the sight of so many bombed-out cities and towns and so many desperate people. Would the world ever be safe again?

I searched the crowds for familiar faces but I did not

talk about myself, nor did I ask about Larissa. Luka was also quiet. We had learned the hard way that we had to be very careful when it came to asking questions about our loved ones.

At each camp we reached, we'd stand in the food lineup and listen to the gossip. It was a way to find what the Soviets were up to and how the different camps were dealing with the issue of forcing refugees to go back to the Soviet Union. Once we had caught up on the news and filled our stomachs, we could go to the camp entrance. Luka would stand watch and I would carefully go through all of the fluttering papers — the wishes and missives of lost loved ones.

Once, my heart nearly stopped when I found a note signed *Raisa Barukovich from Kyiv.*

"Luka . . . " My hand trembled with excitement as I held the paper out to him. "Is your mother's name Raisa?"

"Yes," he said, snatching the note. But as he read it, his face sagged in disappointment. "This isn't my mother's handwriting."

"Maybe someone wrote it for her."

His face lit up with the possibility, but as he read further, the hope was extinguished. He crushed the note and threw it onto the ground.

"It's not my mother." His voice was flat. "Wrong street address, wrong details. Barukovich is a common name in Kyiv. So is Raisa."

I picked the note out of the dust and smoothed it back out. "This may not be your mother," I said as I pinned it back onto the wall. "But she's *someone's* loved one."

Luka sighed. "You're right, Lida. I shouldn't have thrown it down like that."

Weeks later, we shared a campfire and tea with a Czech woman and her two children. The toddler had dark eyebrows and brown eyes like her mother but the older child was a fair-cheeked, flaxen-haired boy who pushed the woman away when she tried to comfort him. Without thinking, I sat close to where he was and quietly hummed a lullaby. He stopped fidgeting and cocked his head to listen. Moments later, he walked over and sat down by my feet. As I hummed, he hummed along, raising his left hand to wipe a tear from his cheek as he did so. I noticed a black mark on the inner part of his wrist.

"You've got a bug there," I said. "Let me brush it off."

The boy looked up at me, startled, then hid his wrist.

"It's not a bug," said the mother. "It's a tattoo."

I had seen the Auschwitz tattoos but this was something different. And on a child?

I looked up at the mother and saw that her bottom lip trembled. "I found him abandoned at the side of a road," she said. "He was babbling in German but no one knew where he came from."

"What does the tattoo mean?"

"I didn't know at first," said the woman. "But a nurse at one of the camps told me she had seen others with the same mark. They're children who were stolen from their families and adopted by German families. The tattoo is so that they can't entirely blend in. Once the war ended, the families didn't want the children. The nurse said she'd turn a blind eye if I wanted to rescue him. There's no chance of finding his real family, after all."

The mother's words felt like ice piercing my heart. Could *this* be why Larissa had been with that Nazi family?

The possibility sickened me. Would she still be with them now, or had they discarded her like trash now that the war was over? Could she survive on her own? Would she even be able to remember who she really was?

I clutched the crucifix around my neck. "Larissa, Larissa, please be safe."

✦ ✦ ✦

We walked from camp to camp and searched for loved ones for the rest of August and into the fall. I read thousands of notes scrawled on faded bits of paper, but I never found Larissa and Luka couldn't find his mother.

While shivering in line for soup at one of the British camps in November, I listened to snatches of conversation around me.

"They're not forcing people back to the Soviet Union anymore," said a grey-bearded man whose gnarled fingers wrapped around his steaming tin cup.

"The Brits, you mean?" asked a younger man standing in front of him.

"The Americans haven't been sending people back for a few weeks," said the older man. "And now the British won't either."

Chapter Twenty-Four

Fischbeck Camp, British Zone, Germany

It was a relief not to have to run anymore.

The British camp we settled on had many Ukrainians. Despite their pledge not to forcibly repatriate us, I didn't want to take a chance. I told them I was from Lviv. So did Luka.

The year ended and 1946 began. Then '47 and we were still refugees. The camp became our home by default. Where else could we go? No country wanted us.

My nimble hands and keen eyesight ensured me steady work over the years, and I didn't mind being paid in food. Refugees liked to be tidy. They needed to look clean and eager when they went for their interviews with the immigration officers from different countries. I always had a long list of people waiting for my services. I amazed myself at what I could create with the limited materials at hand. Out of old Soviet and Nazi uniforms I fashioned decent suits, coats, skirts and blouses. We never went hungry again.

Luka apprenticed to a German pharmacist in town. It was never his plan to stay in Germany, but he needed to hone a skill to impress the immigration officers.

I tried not to feel discouraged, but it was frustrating to still be on German soil this long after the war. The ramshackle camp school and church looked nearly permanent. We DPs had been at the camp for so long that we put on plays, had elections and a camp newspaper.

Still, no country wanted us. I watched every day as the mail was distributed. I watched people's faces and envied their joy when a loved one was found, or a distant relative in Canada or Britain or America agreed to sponsor a lost soul.

But who would sponsor me, and who would sponsor Luka? We had no family. Sometimes I wondered if the whole camp would empty out and no one would be left here but me and Luka.

✤ ✤ ✤

The Germans were friendly, and many had little to eat and their bombed-out homes were no better than the barracks we lived in. But when I went into town, I looked into the faces of women and children and men. I remembered how they looked at me when I was a slave. I didn't know what they saw when they looked at me now, but they made me uneasy.

I always searched the faces of blond girls in town and I always dreamed of finding Larissa. One day, I made up my mind to tell the woman who visited from the Red Cross everything that I suspected. I told her about seeing a girl who looked like Larissa with that Nazi family. I told her about the flaxen-haired boy with the black mark on his wrist.

"You think the same thing might have happened to your sister?"

I didn't reply right way, but finally I said, "Yes."

Then the woman sighed. "It could be very difficult to find her if she can't remember her past. All we can do is look out for a blond girl with blue eyes who looks like she was born in about 1938. We will do our best."

Epilogue

1951

I cherish my barracks room with its flush toilet down the hallway and a kitchen I share with just a few. It is so much more spacious than what I had as an Ostarbeiter.

After a long day of sewing, I walk to a grassy area and sit on a tree stump to watch the children play. There is a lilac bush growing behind the stump and its scent envelops me in memory.

I reach up and touch the cross around my neck and remember the happy times when my parents were alive. In my heart I'm sure that Larissa lives. I would have felt it if she'd died. But the Red Cross has been looking for her for years, and have found no trace.

How I wish there was some way to find her. Should I forget her? Even if I could, the mere scent of lilac would bring her memory back.

I stand up and stretch, then walk back to my barracks.

Luka sits on the bench in front of my building. In his hands is a thick envelope.

"Where did you get that?"

He smiles. "The usual way. It's for you."

He doesn't give it to me right away. He has an odd look on his face. I wonder if the letter is from Zenia in Haifa or Natalia in Montreal.

"It's from Canada," he says, placing it on my out-stretched palm. "A place called Brantford."

I look at the return address. The name is not familiar.

I sit down beside Luka and rip the envelope open. A sprig of lilac falls out. I catch my breath.

I pull out the sheets and unfold them. Paper-clipped to the front page is a photo of a girl. Her hair is woven into two tight braids and she sits between a dark-haired man and woman. He is not the Nazi officer named Franz that I had seen at the bombing. She is not the blond woman from the car. These people are strangers to me. They look kind. Who are they and why are they with Larissa?

"That has to be your sister," said Luka. "She looks so much like you."

This *is* Larissa. The set of her mouth, the look in her eye. And that sprig of lilac. She remembers!

I read:

Dear Lida,

I hope I have finally found you. I think I saw you during the war. Was that you with the OST badge outside the burning factory? I wanted to run to you but they wouldn't let me. Please tell me I've found you.

I have been searching nearly a year, writing the Red Cross, praying for news that you survived the war.

I live in Canada now with my adopted parents,

*Marusia and Ivan Kravchuk. They call me Nadia. That is
a long story, but please know that I am safe and I am
loved and I miss you so much.*

*I have so much to tell you, dear Lida. And questions to
ask. But there is one thing that I would like to ask you
now:*

*Would you like to immigrate to Canada? Marusia and
Ivan will sponsor you.*

*Please write back to me at this address. I will pray every
day for a letter.*

I miss you and I love you.
Larissa

I hold the letter to my heart and tears stream down my
face. Larissa, I didn't find you, but you found me. I could
nearly burst with joy.

Luka's arms wrap around me. I open my eyes and look
at him. He is smiling but I can tell that he is afraid.

"What good news," he says. "Now you can leave this
place."

I brush a bit of wild hair away from his eye. "So can
you. Where I go, you go."

Author's Note

Few people know about the slave raids that Hitler conducted throughout the Soviet Union during World War II. Nazi soldiers would descend upon a town or village and capture the young people who gathered together in public places. The prisoners were loaded into boxcars and transported to Germany, where they were forced to work under brutal conditions. There were between 3 and 5.5 million Ostarbeiters. Most of them were Ukrainian. Many were worked or starved to death.

The Nazis preferred the slave labourers to be in their late teens or early twenties, but there are documented cases of Ostarbeiters who were even younger than Lida. Captured children under twelve were usually either sent directly to death camps or used for medical experiments. It was a rare child who could prove her usefulness and survive.

After the war, Stalin demanded that Soviet citizens captured by the Nazis be returned to the Soviet Union. Those who did return were either killed outright or sent to brutal work camps in Siberia, because Stalin considered anyone who was captured by the Nazis to be a Nazi. Those who managed to escape to the West hid their wartime experiences because they feared being sent back to the Soviet Union. These stories have only begun to emerge since the 1991 dissolution of the Soviet Union.

Sincere thanks to the many former slave labourers who shared their personal stories with me. This book is dedicated to Anelia V., whose detailed recall of day-to-day life as a Nazi slave helped me create an accurate world for Lida.